a novel

D0823100

Other books in the Soul Surfer Series:

Nonfiction:
Body & Soul
Rise Above: A 90-Day Devotional
Ask Bethany, Updated Edition

Fiction:
Clash (Book One)
Burned (Book Two)
Storm (Book Three)
Crunch (Book Four)

a novel

By Rick Bundschuh
Inspired by Bethany Hamilton

For Von, Eddie, Maggie, Aaron, Efren,
and the rest of the crew who give
of their lives and hearts to
"the least of these"

ZONDERKIDZ

Crunch
Copyright © 2007 by Bethany Hamilton
Illustrations © 2007 by Taia Morley

Requests for information should be addressed to:

Zonderkidz, 3900 Sparks Dr., Grand Rapids, Michigan 49546

ISBN 978-0-310-74539-6

Cover design: Cindy Davis
Cover illustration: Taia Morley
Interior design: Christine Orejuela-Winkelman

Printed in the United States of America

15 16 17 18 19 20 21 22 /QG/ 17 16 15 14 13 12 11 10 9 8 7 6 5 4 3 2

Introduction

Although this story is fiction, the situation for the orphans described in this story is very real. Bethany and her family have firsthand experience reaching out to children across our US/Mexico border—in towns large and small.

They could tell you that going to these places isn't always easy, but it *is* always an adventure.

It is Bethany's hope and mine that you will take the opportunity to embark on an adventure much like the one you will be reading about. Trust me, you won't regret it.

God has a special place in his heart for those who are forgotten or neglected by the rest of the world: the poor, the downcast, the weak, and the sick. In James 1:27, the Bible tells us that an important part of God's understanding of religions is that we take care of those who can't take care of themselves. It's his deepest desire that they be helped so that they won't ever have to go to bed hungry, wet, or cold again.

So, why doesn't he just help them, you ask? Well, he does—through us. His word to us couldn't be any clearer.

> This is how we know what love is: Jesus Christ laid down his life for us. And we ought to lay down our lives for our brothers. If anyone has material possessions and sees his brother in need but has no pity on him, how can the love of God be in him?
>
> —1 John 3:16–17

With a little sacrifice on our part, we can actually make another person's life a little better, warmer, fuller, cleaner, or safer.

I encourage you to join your church on a mission trip. Or help put one together if it's never been done before at your church! You will be amazed, just as Bethany was when she realized she was given back far more than she ever gave.

If you aren't able to travel, a little money from babysitting or other jobs, recycled cans, or your allowance can be used to help support a child somewhere in a poverty-stricken corner of the world. Organizations like Compassion International or World Vision are great places to start.

Of course, it is easier to do nothing. To just put it out of our minds. But where would the world be if everyone thought like that? Where would *you* be if you were sick, hungry, cold, or homeless, and no one reached out to help you?

This is a question that Bethany asks herself during this new journey ... but it's the answer she receives that is one you will never forget.

Enjoy the trip!
Rick Bundschuh

Bethany felt a jolt of nervous excitement as the airplane's tires hit the runway in Los Angeles. Then she glanced at the bundle of nerves sitting in the seat next to her and grinned. If there was *anyone* who understood how she was feeling at that moment, it was Holly Silva. They not only surfed together and trained together, they also survived cliff-hanging rescues together. And *that* was a bonding moment if there ever was one.

"So, what do you think?"

Holly gave her a shaky grin. "Guess I was having a hard time believing this was for real, until now."

"Yeah ... I still can't believe we're finally on our first mission trip," Bethany said, filled with awe as she scanned the other excited faces on the plane. The usual suspects were there: Malia, Jenna, and Monica were craning their necks to catch a glimpse of Bethany and Holly who sat a couple of rows behind. They spotted them and waved wildly, causing them to laugh.

"All of us in Mexico. This is going to be crazy!" Bethany shook her head.

"Good crazy, right?" Holly asked tentatively, and they both laughed again as Bethany continued to look around.

Black spiky hair gave Kai's location away as he gabbed with his buddies, including Dano, a large teenager with cool tribal tattoos. *A giant heart to match too*, Bethany thought, remembering how hard he had worked on the fund-raisers.

Kai said something that brought a roar of laughter from the guys, and Bethany couldn't help smiling to herself. *Not exactly your typical church youth group*, she thought. But then, that was kind of the cool thing about their group.

None of them were exactly typical.

Oh, there were some like her who came from strong Christian families, but the majority of teens peering out the windows of the 747 at the orange lights flickering from the "City of Angels" were from homes where the name of Christ was more likely used in a curse than in praise.

But that didn't seem to stop them from reaching out to God—something she could totally identify with.

Kai and Dano had been drawn to their group by the wild and crazy game night Sarah and her staff had put together, but they stayed because somewhere along the way they found out Jesus was for real.

Bethany smiled to herself, remembering how blown away they all were the day their miracle financial gift appeared, allowing them to go on this mission trip.

After countless car washes and even after her crazy idea of a surf-a-thon with inflatable toys, they were still such a long way off from what they needed that a lot of them wondered if the mission trip was really going to happen. And then God showed up in his perfect time to make it possible.

No one had any doubts after that happened that God was behind them on the trip—or that he was paving the way for something good to happen.

The Fasten Seat Belt signs turned off overhead, and she and Holly, along with everyone else on the plane, scrambled for their carry-on bags.

"Okay, everyone, stick together and meet us at the gate!" Sarah, their youth director, called out before she followed her assistants, Mike and Gabe, off the plane.

"I wonder what it's going to be like," Holly said as the group fanned out along the boarding tunnel. Bethany glanced over at her. Short, trendy hair, just a touch of lipstick (a recent victory in her makeup battle with her mom)—Holly looked cute and sure of herself, but Bethany knew Holly was just as nervous as she was ... if not more.

"Guess we'll find out soon enough," Bethany smiled, trying to sound more confident than she felt.

"Ghettos aren't pretty, that's for sure," Jenna said.

"I hear some of the stuff we're going to do is pretty harsh," Malia said as she slung a backpack over her shoulder.

"Great!" Monica said, giving her new manicure a worried look.

"Well, *I'm* game," Bethany announced.

"When *aren't you* game?" Kai teased, looking over his shoulder as they entered the terminal. "Car washes, surf-a-thons ..." He glanced over at Dano and winked. "No telling what she'll come up with for us to do in Mexico."

"Be afraid," Holly said with a mischievous grin.

"*Very* afraid," Bethany added, and they all laughed.

Thirty minutes later, they were piling into the three vans idling by the curb in the early-morning light. Sarah, Mike, and Gabe were in the drivers' seats.

In spite of the all-night flight, Bethany found her mind racing, wondering about the week to come. Unlike her friends, whose heads were already bobbing back to sleep as soon as the vans hit the interstate, she had slept through most of the flight. She was used to traveling at odd hours for surf competitions.

She turned and squinted out the window at the California scenery flashing by. She thought about Sarah's description of some of the work they would be doing in the ghettos that lined the deep hills and gullies around Tijuana: building small houses, bathing children from areas without running water, playing with orphans, and handing out food and clothes.

More scenery flashed by as Bethany stared out the window and thought about Jesus' words: "When you help them, you help me." She thought how cool it was that Jesus wanted the world to know how much he loved people who were, for the most part, forgotten or ignored.

She knew God had given her a heart that wanted to reach out to people. She just hoped she measured up now that she was in the position to help.

Bethany suddenly sat up straight as the Pacific Ocean came into view. "That's Trestles!" she said excitedly, elbowing Holly. "They're holding the nationals there this week."

"Wha—?" Holly mumbled groggily.

Kai cracked an eye open and asked, "So, why aren't you there? Or is that a sore subject?"

"Not *too* sore," Bethany admitted with an unconvincing grin.

"All things work together for good, right?" Malia said with a sleepy, but warm smile. Bethany glanced over at her, remembering their surf trip in Samoa.

"Yeah … if I had qualified, I wouldn't be on this trip."

"Could've saved us a lot of work," Kai said, grinning at Dano. But Dano was still sleeping soundly.

Soon the others fell back to sleep, and Bethany continued to watch the California coastline as the vans continued south toward San Diego and the Mexican border.

By the time they reached the United States-Mexico border, most of the kids were awake. The border crossing went pretty smoothly, but the sudden change at the border from the US side to the hardscrabble town pressed up against the edge of a large steel fence shocked many of the kids into silence.

It seems like we've stepped into another world, Bethany thought. With no trees and with cement everywhere, it looked so barren. But almost immediately they entered the busy city traffic of Tijuana.

"Whoa! This is *nuts!*" Sarah said about the crazy traffic. Cars zoomed around her on both sides, while she tried to keep up with Mike and Gabe in the vans ahead. She glanced in the rearview mirror with an exasperated sigh.

"Hey, Sarah, maybe you should let me take over from here," Kai suggested.

"Or me," Dano piped up. "I know all about nuts."

"Uh-huh," Sarah smiled, trying to keep her eyes on the road.

"Yeah, they're real experts," Bethany added, trying to keep a straight face as they bantered back and forth.

They flashed past dozens of tiny eateries and stands that sold anything you could imagine, from fresh spices to wild-looking guitars to jewelry, clothes, and beautiful pottery. People were everywhere. Color was everywhere. Bethany spotted an enormous fruit market and felt her mouth water.

"If we get the chance, I'm so there," Bethany said.

"Look at those cool skirts!" Holly said.

"Where?" Monica asked, practically trying to crawl over Malia and Jenna for a peek. The girls groaned in unison and then laughed.

"Monica, you're too much," Jenna chuckled.

"What? So I like clothes. What girl doesn't?"

"This isn't exactly going to be fashion week in New York," Bethany teased as the vans turned down an old dusty road, slowing to a stop in front of a slightly crumbling but tidy-looking two-story building.

"Not exactly Kansas either, Dorothy," Kai said under his breath as they all took in the iron bars on every window. A wild-looking dog peered at them from the side of the dusty, dinged up SUV parked next to the building.

"Wow," Bethany said, feeling her nervousness return as she looked at the poverty around them. She felt her spirits rise again at the sight of a friendly looking couple exiting the house to greet them.

"Okay, gang, let's go meet our hosts," Sarah said with a smile as she pulled her keys from the ignition.

"Come on, Toto," Bethany called over her shoulder to Kai as she, Holly, and the other girls scrambled for the door. Dano's laughter followed them out of the van.

Eddie and Maggie Passmore were about as nice as you could get, Bethany thought as Maggie pulled away from hugging her and Eddie grabbed her hand in a warm, energetic handshake. She'd been the last in line for the welcome, but they didn't seem to have lost their enthusiasm.

"So, are you ready for the tour?" Eddie asked with a broad smile.

"Oh, she's ready," Kai said dryly as Eddie led them into a large room filled with a mismatch of used sofas and chairs parked on a worn but clean carpet.

"Our strategy room," Eddie provided. "It's not exactly the Hilton, but it works."

"What made you pick Mexico?" Bethany asked as he led them out of the main room to the lower part of the dorm that held the office and a kitchen large enough for visiting groups to prepare meals.

"I first visited here when I was a teenager," he replied, glancing around at the group. "Probably about Kai and Dano's age—you two are about sixteen, right?" The boys nodded. "It really got in my blood. I mean, no matter where I went after that, through college to being a youth pastor ... I just couldn't get these people out of my mind. The next time I visited with Maggie, God opened the doors for us in such a big way that there was no doubt *where* he wanted us." Eddie smiled and shook his head, giving Maggie a look that said it still amazed him.

"Let's show them where they'll be sleeping," Maggie said with a smile of her own as she led the tired but curious group upstairs.

The upper part of the dorm was divided into two large sleeping areas; one for guys and one for girls, with shower facilities for both. Duffel bags began to drop around them like flies as Bethany and the girls rushed to claim the bunks they wanted. They laughed, hearing the commotion from the boys' side. They could hear Mike say, "Come on, guys, age has priority!"

"How much you want to bet Dano gets whatever bunk he wants?" Bethany grinned.

"If I was as big as a giant, I know I'd get the bunk I wanted," Holly said as she flopped onto her bed. "I feel like I could sleep forever."

"Me too," Malia yawned.

"Not me," Monica said. "This neighborhood makes me nervous."

"Getting your nails done makes you nervous," Jenna said, and Monica threw a pillow at her.

"Well, there's no way I can sleep yet. I'm going to see if I can find Sarah," Bethany said, rising from her bunk.

"Don't volunteer me for anything crazy until you, like, *ask* me first," Holly called after her as she headed for the door.

"That goes double for the rest of us," Malia said, getting nods of agreement from Jenna and Monica.

"Are you talking to me?" Bethany said as she blinked innocently and then hurried to shut the door behind her before anyone could respond.

Chuckling to herself, she jogged down the stairs, turned the corner, and almost ran right into Eddie as he rounded the corner from the opposite direction. They both laughed.

"Almost a head-on collision," Eddie said, grinning.

"Oh man, you aren't kidding!" She glanced behind Eddie. "I was looking for Sarah. Have you seen her?"

Eddie nodded. "As a matter of fact, Maggie took her on a tour of the neighborhood."

"I was going to ask her if we could go running tomorrow morning."

"You mean your whole group?"

"Well, probably just us girls," Bethany said, then chewed on her lip thoughtfully. "Or at the very least, me and Holly." She grinned inwardly. *Sorry, Holly!*

"You're a surfer, right?"

"Yeah," Bethany nodded shyly. "I kind of like to keep up on my training." She left out the part about running helping her nerves over the mission trip.

"Nothing wrong with that," Eddie said amiably. "I used to run myself—though it's been a while." He patted his stomach, and Bethany smiled.

"Tell you what: it's not that great of a neighborhood for you girls to go running in alone. But if you really want to go, I'll come around 6:30 a.m. and run with you."

"Really? You don't mind?"

"Maggie will thank you; she's been after me to get back into running. I'm still carrying around all the stuff I ate at Christmastime."

"Okay then, it's a deal," Bethany said happily. "I'll set the alarm on my watch."

"Don't forget the time change. And I'll bring the stick."

"A stick? What for?"

"Ah, if you're going to go for a jog around here, carrying a stick with you is a good idea."

"For muggers?" Bethany asked worriedly. Holly might forgive her for an early morning run, but not for a mugger.

"Yeah ... the *four-legged* kind," Eddie laughed. "The stray dogs around here can sometimes get a little too close for comfort."

Bethany nodded casually, but her mind raced. *What have I got us into now, Holly?* she thought

with a twinge of doubt—not just about the run—
but the whole trip. Then she remembered her dad's
words just before she got on the plane: "Just trust
in God and let him lead you, Bethany. He's the best
father any of us could ever imagine having."

"Papa!"

Eduardo shot up from the pallet he had been
sleeping on and looked around. It was dark, but he
knew if he reached out his arm he could touch the
cot his mother and sister slept on, knew that the
other two cots his four brothers shared would be
just beyond that. He put his hand to his chest, feeling his heart still racing from the dream. And what
a good dream it was!

He had been running down a beautiful soccer field. So much green! He had never seen that
much green in one place. He grinned to himself,
remembering how he scored a goal for his team
and how good it felt when his teammates thumped
his back with congratulations. His smile faded as
he recalled searching for his father's face in the
stand filled with people.

For just a moment, he thought he'd spotted
him when he saw a man stand up and begin to
walk toward him through the crowd. But people
kept getting in his way, and no matter how hard
Eduardo squinted, he couldn't make out the
man's face.

Eduardo shivered but resisted the urge to crawl onto his mother's cot. If his brothers woke up and saw him there, he would never hear the end of it. They would say he was *loco* to dream that he would do anything other than rummage through other people's garbage. They would also say that he was a baby to call out to a father he had never had.

Eduardo grimaced and curled up on his pallet again. He wasn't a baby. He was five years old—old enough to know better than to wake his mother, and old enough to know he needed some sleep before he had to get up and go to work again.

Still, he thought as his eyes began to grow heavy with sleep, it would have been nice if he could have seen that man's face. It would be nice to at least *pretend* he had a father.

two

"That's weird," Bethany said, trying to catch her breath as she and Holly ended their run at the empty space where their van had been parked. "I wonder who left so early?"

"I don't know," Holly gasped, holding her side. "I didn't think there was anyone besides you who was crazy enough to get up this early."

"I thought you girls needed a jogging companion, not a racing competitor," panted an older voice. Bethany and Holly laughed as they spotted Eddie heading toward them in a slow, weary trot.

"We only sprinted the last block when we saw we were back at the dorm," Bethany grinned. "Thanks for running with us; we wouldn't have felt safe without you."

"Oh, you're welcome," Eddie said as he bent over to catch his breath. "This was a good wake-up call for me. I am *so* out of shape!"

"I shoulda warned you about her," Holly chuckled. "It's never a run; it's always a race!"

"Hey, did you three enjoy your morning jog around luxurious Tijuana?" Sarah grinned as she stepped onto the porch of the dorm wearing sweat-pants and a sweatshirt to ward off the cool morning air. In her hand was a large mug of steaming coffee.

Sarah started to say something else when Bethany saw her eyes dart to the empty spot where the van had been.

"Eddie, where's the van?"

"I don't have any idea," Eddie said, suddenly glancing around. "Did one of your drivers take the kids somewhere?"

"No, the drivers are inside having breakfast!" Sarah said with the start of panic in her voice.

"Uh-oh."

Bethany and Holly looked at each other. They didn't like the sound of the "uh-oh" or the sudden creepy thought that someone dangerous could be nearby.

Sarah hurried back into the dorm, and Eddie, wiping his forehead on his sleeve, followed behind her.

"This is *not* good," Bethany whispered to Holly as they quickly followed them inside.

"Okay, guys, the blue van is missing," Sarah announced as she entered the dining room. "Did anyone see anyone strange around the dorm this morning?"

Eyes darted back and forth. A few kids shrugged. Bethany noticed that Monica, Jenna, and Malia were speechless for once as they stared back at Sarah with wide eyes.

"Oh, man. I knew you should've let me be in charge of the van," Dano said, trying to lighten the mood. Kai elbowed him and gave him a dark, brotherly scowl before he turned to look at Bethany and Holly.

"You guys didn't see anything on your run?" Kai asked Bethany and Holly. They shook their heads.

"Wait a minute. I have the keys," Sarah said, glancing at Eddie. "How could the van be gone?"

"Hate to say it, but the thieves in this part of the neighborhood can be very resourceful," Eddie replied sadly. "They can bypass ignition systems with just a screwdriver and a wire cutter."

"They took a *rental* van!" Mike exclaimed, frustrated.

"Do you have insurance?" Eddie asked.

"Yeah, both here and in the States," Sarah said slowly, pursing her lips. Bethany knew she was trying to come up with some sort of plan.

"You know, I can't help thinking that we can make something good come out of this," Eddie said. "Maggie and I always seem to get hit with something crazy just before God leads us to someone in need."

Trust in God and let him lead you. Bethany heard her dad's voice whisper through her mind. In spite of her fears of the unknown, she said a quick prayer that God would lead Sarah—would lead them all—to wherever it was that they needed to be.

"Okay," Sarah said finally. "We might have to cram people in or shuttle, but I think we should try to stick with our plans."

"That's the spirit!" Eddie smiled. "I think this would be a good time for us to pray."

"A five-minute time limit for showers is *crazy*," Monica grumbled as she strolled into their dorm room with a towel on her head.

"From the wettest place on earth to the driest place on earth," Jenna said, digging through her duffel bag.

"Well, like Kai says, we aren't in Kansas any- more," Bethany said as she sat on her cot, drying her hair with a beach towel.

"Or Hawaii," Holly interjected. "I can't remember ever hearing about a car being stolen back home."

"That's because we live on an *island*." Bethany laughed. "My mom says if our car was ever stolen, we'd just sit in the Wal-Mart parking lot. Sooner or later the thief would have to drive by."

The girls all laughed.

"Is there anyone else that is creeped out by this besides me?" Monica asked.

"I am," Jenna answered truthfully.

"Me too," Malia said.

"I'm kind of creeped out," Holly admitted slowly as she glanced at Bethany. "I keep wondering how we're going to do anything good if stuff like this keeps happening."

Bethany nodded. "Yeah, I was kind of thinking the same thing. But then I thought about what Eddie said, and I have this gut feeling that he's right about something good being on the other side. Think about it. Most of the people we've listened to who've gone on mission trips have stories of tough stuff happening. But they trusted God and kept going. They all thought the trip was worth the hard stuff."

"Remember when I got hurt on our trip to Samoa?" Malia said. "If that hadn't happened, you probably never would've talked to Liam about God."

Bethany's eyes lit up. "Yeah! And how about when we first met Jenna? If I had ignored what God was trying to tell me, we wouldn't all be friends right now!"

"And I would've probably drowned," Jenna added.

"And our cliff adventure," Holly reminded them. "We wouldn't be here now if it weren't for those people we helped."

Bethany grinned, feeling their excitement return with each memory, and she recalled a verse Sarah liked to quote: "And they overcame him by the blood of the Lamb and the word of their testimony."

"Geez, Bethany, I never noticed how much Rip Curl stuff you have," Jenna said, suddenly plopping down on the bunk as she rifled through Bethany's duffel bag. "Rip Curl duffle bag, Rip Curl daypack, Rip Curl sweatshirt ..."

"Well, she is sponsored by Rip Curl," Malia said dramatically.

"Too bad they don't make makeup," Holly said, and they all laughed.

"How about money?" Monica asked. "Have they started giving you money to surf?"

"Only pros get money from their sponsors," Bethany answered, pulling her long blonde hair into a ponytail. "I haven't gone pro yet, so I get free stuff and my travel expenses paid for."

"How much free stuff?" Monica pressed, and everyone groaned. "How are they going to know if she wears all of that—or if she gives it to her friends to wear?" Monica asked defensively.

"The point is, I agreed to represent them in contests *and* by wearing their clothing," Bethany explained. "It's not about what they do or don't find out, it's about my word. I gave my word."

"Yeah, well what they don't know won't hurt them," Monica said with a small smile.

"No, you don't get it, Monica. It's about my honesty and making sure that if I make a promise I keep it, even if there is no contract or anything in writing."

"Nobody does that, Bethany. That's why there are stacks of contracts and lawyers for everything," Monica said, exasperated. But her eyes said something else, Bethany thought. Almost like she wanted what Bethany said to be true—that people really did keep their promises.

A call to gather in the main room interrupted the conversation and the girls left their dorm room to join the others downstairs.

As they entered the room, Bethany glanced at the bars covering the windows and, for the first time since they arrived, was glad they were there. She spotted Kai slouched low next to Dano on one of the sofas. He slid his eyes from her to the bars and back to her with a look that said he was thinking the same thing.

"Okay, the good news is that since we were insured, the theft of the van is covered," Sarah announced as she looked around the room. "The bad news is that it will take Mike all day to get the paperwork straightened out and to rent us another vehicle. So, we're going to have to do some reshuffling for today."

Hands popped up all around.

"Did you call the police?"

"Yes, right away. Eddie has already talked to them."

"Do they think they'll be able to find the van?"

"They aren't real optimistic. Eddie thinks it's probably being painted another color at this very moment," Sarah said with a "what are you going to do?" shrug. "So, our new plan for today is that those of you who rode in my van will go by cab to an orphanage and provide the kids with some Hawaiian entertainment."

"Define *entertainment*," Bethany said with a wary note to her voice, and everyone laughed—including Sarah.

"Well, I've asked Kai to play his ukulele, so I need any of you who know how to hula to jump on that team with him. If you can think of anything uniquely Hawaiian we can add to the mix, jump in now."

"How about something on surfing?" Monica suggested.

"Kinda hard to show and tell without an ocean," Sarah said.

"Bethany has a video of her surfing. You should make her go and explain it," Holly interjected with a grin in Bethany's direction that said "gotcha."

Bethany took it in stride; she had volunteered Holly for way more than a video show. Besides, she was still trying to picture Kai playing a ukulele. She raised her eyebrows at him, and he gave her a good-natured scowl.

"Bethany?"

"Okay. I do have the video my brother shot at the Pine Trees contest. It's on my iPod."

"The kids would probably love to see something like that—if you're willing," Sarah said, adding a charming smile to the request.

"I'll do it," Bethany grinned back. "I have the plug-ins if they have the TV."

"Eddie?"

"It works as long as the city power is on."

"Okay, those of you who are going to the orphanage meet with me. The rest of you will be helping to build houses this morning. Make sure only to bring with you what you need. Don't bring anything you are not willing to part with. Eddie says we'll be in a part of town where things might get stolen."

A burst of movement followed as everyone scrambled to get their gear together.

Since Bethany already had her iPod, she opted to sit on the steps with Sarah and watch Eddie's group load the trailer with lumber and supplies.

"I've never built a house before," tall, skinny Ben was saying as he slid some lumber into the trailer.

"Me neither," his friend Jeff said with an excited grin.

"If you can swing a hammer and hit the nail—at least most of the time—you will be fine," Eddie said.

"Why would anyone want to live in a house we made?" asked Ben.

"The people we're building for are people who have run out of options," Eddie explained. "You will find them extremely grateful that they get a roof over their heads and a place to call their own—even if it is a rough, ten-by-ten-foot room."

"Ten-by-ten-foot? That's not a house; that's a storage shed!"

"It's a lot more than they have now," Eddie said over his shoulder as he went for another armload of lumber.

Bethany glanced at Sarah. "I was really hoping we would be helping build some homes today too," she admitted as she continued to watch Eddie's team. "But I keep reminding myself that there's got to be a reason our plans were changed—that since God's in charge, he allowed this to happen for a reason."

"That's exactly how I'm looking at it too," Sarah said, putting her arm around Bethany's shoulder. "The minute I realized we would have to settle for a cab—something that we couldn't load lumber in—I just knew God had different plans for us today. And then Eddie suggested the orphanage."

"Kind of like following along with a really good mystery, huh?" Bethany said with a small smile, reminding Sarah of a story she had told them not long ago.

"Exactly!" Sarah grinned. "You never know how it's going to turn out until you get to the end of the book."

"Ever wish you could turn to the last page for a little peek?" Bethany asked.

Sarah laughed out loud. "Always! But then that would kind of spoil the mystery, wouldn't it?"

"Yeah," Bethany nodded. But she still couldn't help wondering what lay ahead for them—and what was so important that God had decided to change their plans.

Eduardo couldn't believe his eyes. He had only been working for a couple of hours when he found a large, clear trash bag filled with shiny pots and pans. Expensive ones at that! *Heavy too*, he thought as he dragged the bag down the slope of the trash heap toward his home.

"Where do you think you're going?" his brother Manuel called out to him as he looked up from his spot with narrowed eyes.

Eduardo ignored him and kept pulling the bag, yelling for his mother as soon as he saw he was close enough for her to hear him. She hurried out the door with his baby sister on her hip, eyes wide with worry until she realized that he wasn't hurt.

"Oh!" she exclaimed as she spotted his find. He grinned proudly as she rushed over and studied the contents of the bag. "You are such a good boy—eyes like an eagle!"

"We can sell these for good money?" Eduardo asked.

"Yes," his mother said, lovingly brushing his hair back from his face. "This will be a big help—so big that I think you deserve to take the rest of the day off."

Eduardo was so elated that tears of gratitude sprang to his eyes. He quickly blinked them back. "So I can go?"

"Yes," his mother said, laughing as she watched him spring into action and run across the tiny compound. "But Eduardo, come back, okay?" she called after him. "I really need you with me!"

"I'll be back, Mama," he called over his shoulder. "I promise!"

And he would be back. He loved his mother. He had told her about his dream, and she hadn't made fun of him. Instead, she had suggested that the man he had thought was his father may have been God. Eduardo had thought about God all morning, even prayed for God to help him. And look what happened! It was like the miracles they spoke of at the orphanage.

Eduardo picked up his pace, running as fast as his five-year-old legs would carry him. He had so many questions—but one in particular that he just *had* to find the answer to.

three

"There he is!" Maggie announced from behind Bethany. Bethany turned to check out their new ride.

It was a green, dented-up, older model station wagon with the word *Taxi* written in bright yellow, but very large, old-English-style script on each front door.

The driver looked to be in his early twenties and wore a Yankees baseball cap turned backward on his head. He smiled at Sarah and the teens as they climbed into the station wagon.

"Maggie, please tell Miguel we really appreciate him agreeing to this at the last moment," Sarah said as she closed the door.

Maggie translated in rapid Spanish, and Miguel replied. "He says that he is grateful for the work," Maggie said, then added, "Miguel is part of our Bible study group. He has four children, so we try to give him work whenever we can."

"Well, it looks like God is working this trip out for everyone," Sarah said.

As the taxi turned onto the traffic-congested paved highway, Bethany studied the landscape around her. The contrast to her island home was extreme. While thick green foliage was the norm in Hawaii, in this busy city there was hardly a blade of grass—only buildings crowding each other, vying for visitors' attention. At home, massive trees gave shade and beauty everywhere you went, but here the few trees Bethany spotted were stunted and gray.

The brightly colored buildings, closely packed homes, and loud cars mixed with the smell of burning trash and exhaust fumes to assault her senses.

From an island with a little more than fifty thousand residents to a sprawling city of over a million, the change for Bethany and her friends was enormous.

And then there was the poverty.

As they drove out of the touristy part of the city, Bethany could see shacks built into the hillside made of scrap lumber and aluminum siding with dirt-filled tires serving as steps. At first she thought they were just storage sheds, but as she looked closer it became obvious that these were incredibly small, ramshackle *homes* clinging desperately to the dusty hillside. All signs of plant life seemed ripped out of the ground.

Bethany's attention was suddenly drawn away by the sound of Maggie's voice.

"I'd like to tell you all a little about the orphanage we are visiting," she began. "First of all, this is an all-boy orphanage. Many times you will find that orphanages in Mexico are like this—all-boy or all-girl. Also, many of the kids aren't *true* orphans. Most have at least one parent alive, so it is more accurate to say that we are going to a home for unwanted, abused, or poverty-stricken kids. They're young but have had tough lives already. Some have been buying and selling drugs for their parents. Many have seen violence, sexual abuse, and other things children should never be exposed to.

"At the orphanage, we teach the children about God by caring for them and giving them food, shelter, clothing, safety, and schooling.

"Since there are so many kids for so few adults, you will find them starved for human attention. So, don't let it bother you if the younger ones want to be carried or touched."

Bethany and the rest of the team looked at each other silently, trying to imagine what it would feel like to go through such horrors—at such a young age.

"Can they be adopted?" Bethany asked when she found her voice again.

"Well, technically the true orphans can. But it is pretty hard to do in Mexico," Maggie replied. "People ask that all the time though, and some really find their hearts going out to a particular kid and want to take him or her home. But it can't be done easily or with most kids."

"So, what happens to them?" Kai asked.

"Ah, that's another tragic part of their story," Maggie said sadly. "The parents usually come back to claim their child when the kid is old enough to work in the streets. We often run into the kids on the street … it's not a pretty sight."

"There ought to be a law against that," Monica said from the other side of Bethany.

"Well, you will find that things are done a lot differently here than they are in the United States," Maggie said with a sigh.

No kidding, Bethany thought. Even though the team had been through an orientation meeting before going on the trip, nothing had prepared them for this—for the cruel realities of children living in the grip of poverty.

The orphanage was nestled in a residential neighborhood. The two-story, bright pink building was surrounded by a large wall, the top of which was imbedded with glass and barbed wire.

Looks more like a prison than an orphanage, Bethany thought with a bit of dismay as the taxi parked in front of the door. She also noticed Kai's tight grip on his ukulele as he studied the hand-printed letters over the entrance that read, "Emmanuel Orphanage." A small frown was forming on his face.

"The kids are expecting us," Maggie said with an encouraging smile as she opened the door of the taxi. "There is no school today, and they rarely get something as exotic as a hula show, so they are really excited."

As if on cue, dozens of small black-haired children rushed out to meet the group as they emerged from the taxi. They tugged on Bethany's shirt, laughing as they grabbed the teens' hands and pulled them toward the gate of the orphanage. Bethany felt her heart melt as the few that surrounded her studied her missing arm with concern, whispering to each other in Spanish before turning back to her with wide, compassionate eyes.

They have it so much harder than I do. How could they feel sorry for me? she thought with amazement.

Maggie bent down and quietly explained something to the kids in their own language.

"*Tiburon*?" One of the little ones asked in disbelief.

"Sí, sí, tiburon," Maggie replied patiently.

Mouths gaping wide, the children passed the word on to the latecomers, each of whom stared at Bethany in awe.

"I explained to them that you are a surfer who lost your arm to a shark," Maggie said almost apologetically. "They're just curious, and they really don't mean any harm by it."

"Sure, that's okay," Bethany said, smiling at the little group before she turned back to Maggie. "It always makes kids curious when they see someone missing an arm."

"They all want to hear what happened, but you don't have to talk about it if you don't want to."

"No, I don't mind at all. I like it when my story encourages others to learn more about God," she said smiling shyly.

Maggie gave her a grateful smile. She turned back to the children—now gathered in a thick group around the team—and explained that they would hear the story of the shark and see something special right from Hawaii.

The children squealed with delight and hurried to lead the team through the gates of the orphanage.

Bethany looked around the large paved play area surrounded by a block wall. A bent basketball hoop minus the net hung from the wall.

A busy kitchen area opened up to a dining room with murals on the walls. The murals showed children doing various activities with words written in Spanish underneath—words that Bethany—with her one semester of instruction in the language— could not make out.

Off the dining room was a small living room containing several well-used sofas and a stained rug over a tiled floor.

The place was tidy and clean, yet it had the feel of a well-used building. Nicks, scratches, and chipped paint were everywhere.

Maggie introduced the team to the directors of the orphanage, Eva and Manuel Ruiz. Then the directors showed them where to set up for their sharing time.

A large TV was brought in for Bethany. She hooked her video iPod into the back and gave it a test run.

Bethany couldn't help feeling her spirits lift as the room soon filled with excited, smiling children.

Maggie located a globe and used it to show the children where the visitors had come from.

Hands shot in the air, and Maggie translated back the questions to the group.

"How did you get here?"

"We flew." Bethany laughed at their confused expressions. "On an airplane!"

The boys giggled.

"How long did it take?"

"A little over five hours," Holly answered.

"What is it like where you live?"

Several teens on the team attempted to explain about a land of green where palm trees dot the beach and where turtles and whales roam the shoreline.

Then Kai was up. He explained that the ukulele was a traditional Hawaiian instrument. Malia jumped in next to describe the hula and to show

how the movement of hands, feet, and body were like beautiful sign language.

Kai promptly began plinking away at a song while Monica, Holly, Jenna, and the rest of the girls danced a hula for the wide-eyed little boys.

A bit self-conscious at first, the girls quickly shook it off and performed as smoothly and beautifully as they were used to at home. When they were done, the children clapped wildly.

Maggie then introduced Bethany and explained that she was a competitive surfer who had overcome a life-threatening event.

Bethany felt uneasy speaking through an interpreter, so she tried to keep her sentences short and to the point.

"What would you like to hear most about surfing?"

"Did it hurt when you were bit by the shark?" a little boy asked in Spanish, and Maggie smiled apologetically.

"It's okay," Bethany said as she nodded. She'd learned enough about human nature to know that, for these little boys, hearing about surfing would only be interesting once their curiosity about the shark attack was satisfied.

"So . . . ," she said, looking down at the eager faces. "Let me tell you about the day I lost my arm."

The children quieted down quickly as Maggie interpreted.

"I started surfing when I was about your age," Bethany continued. "I loved it from the moment I started." She smiled. "My family taught me that there were dangerous things in the water, and that it was possible to get hurt—or even killed. In fact, we knew people who had been attacked by sharks. But like most people, I never thought that it would happen to me."

The children were as silent as stones, their eyes drifting to the empty, knotted sleeve of her shirt as she talked.

"Up to that time, the worst thing that had happened to me while surfing was getting stung by a box jellyfish." Bethany glanced up and noticed Kai was listening as intently as the orphans.

"What is that?" a little boy asked. "What does that feel like?"

Bethany did her best to explain the painful sting from the bizarre creature made up of 99 percent water. "But they don't attack you on purpose," she assured them. "They just float along, and you bump into them because they are mostly underwater and hard to see." Bethany turned to Maggie. "Don't they have jellyfish at the beach here?"

"I am sure they do, but most of these children have never been to the ocean—even though it's only twenty minutes away."

"I wish there was some way to fix that," Bethany said softly. She took a deep breath and then proceeded to tell them of the morning when she and her friends had been surfing and how quickly and without any warning she had been attacked.

"Did it hurt?" "Why didn't it eat *all* of you?" and other similar questions exploded out of the young audience.

"No, strangely enough, it didn't hurt until later," Bethany said. "I felt a tug and a pinch and that was it."

"Show them the picture," Kai prompted.

Bethany grinned at him and pulled a book out of her backpack that showed her standing next to a surfboard with a huge U-shaped bite out of it.

The children gasped before rushing at her with more questions: "Why didn't you bleed to death?" "Who saved you?" "Did they kill the shark?"

Bethany glanced at Maggie who seemed pleased but exhausted from the rapid-fire translations, and moved on to explain how she had been pulled out of trouble by holding on to her friend's dad as he paddled both of them to shore.

She told of her journey to the hospital and how God had helped her heal and given her the strength and ability to continue surfing.

"Aren't you scared? How can you go back in the water again?"

"Most of the time I'm not scared," Bethany answered honestly. "And I trust God. That's how I can go back in the water."

"How can you trust God? Have you ever met him? Have you seen his face?"

Bethany and Maggie both turned to the source of the voice: a little boy standing in the doorway of the room. His hands were clenched at his sides. He was skinny with scratches on his legs and shoes that were so filthy Bethany felt her heart would break.

"I haven't seen his face, but I *have* felt his love and protection," she answered gently. Then, remembering her dad's words, she added, "He's the best father any of us could ever imagine."

The little boy's eyes widened in surprise, but then he thought for a moment and frowned. "I have to see his face," he said and then abruptly ran out of the orphanage.

Bethany turned back to Maggie. "Do you know him? Should we go after him or something?"

"His name is Eduardo. He visits us when he is able." Maggie shook her head. "Most likely he is heading back home ... though I should tell Eddie to check on him. I have never heard him talk that way before."

Bethany looked out the door, pondering on what had just transpired, until she caught sight of another little boy grinning up at her.

"Did they catch the shark?"

She smiled down at him and opened to another page in her book that showed a huge shark being held up by a backhoe.

"They caught it. It was fourteen feet long," said Bethany. Maggie, taking a second to do math in her head, changed the measurement into meters for the group.

"How big *is* that?"

Bethany paced out approximately fourteen feet and said, "From here to there!"

Ooohs and ahhhs filled the room. Holly and the girls gave her a thumbs up.

"You're a hit," Kai said with a teasing grin.

"Yeah, kind of like *Jaws*," Dano added, and they all laughed.

"Speaking of movies," Bethany said, giving Dano a look before turning back to the group, "Would any of you like to see what it's like to surf in Hawaii?"

"Sí! Sí!" The boys clapped excitedly.

"Okay, here we go!" Bethany pushed a button on her iPod, and the screen lit up with surfing action.

"What's all this footage for?" Kai asked as the boys scooted forward quietly, their eyes glued to the TV.

"It's a collection of shots I gave to my sponsor so that they can use it for promotional stuff," Bethany whispered.

"There are some good shots in this," Kai whispered back.

"That's because my brother edited out all the waves where I don't get out of the barrel or land the trick."

"Still, the surfing is great! I didn't know you were that good."

"And I didn't know you could play such a mean ukulele," Bethany laughed. "I ought to get you to record something for my next DVD project."

"That would be cool."

Bethany glanced back to the young faces enraptured by the sight of her image sailing across the powder blue water and wished with all of her heart she could have more than a day with them. She wanted to give them a chance to see the world outside the gates of the orphanage.

They live so close to the ocean, but most of them will never go, she thought sadly.

Suddenly the kids began to squeal and laugh, and her smile returned.

"Ah! The wipeout section," she grinned, glancing to Kai and Dano. "Now you will see my true talent!"

They watched and winced at the footage of her getting clobbered by the lip of a double-overhead wave or being swallowed whole by a racing tube or being air-dropped into oblivion by a late takeoff.

"That must have hurt," Dano said with a note of awe.

"Not too much. But I sure got held under for a long time on a couple of those. Watch, you'll see my board get snapped in two on the next shot."

Ooohs and ahhhs roared out of the kids at each wipeout.

The grand finale was footage that her brother Noah had shot by jumping in the water with the camera just as Bethany had sailed by him. A thin curtain of water covered her. He slowed it way down in editing, ending the film with a ballet of beauty and grace.

Clapping erupted all around the room as the end credits rolled.

"Take me surfing! Take me surfing!" The dark-haired brood chanted in Spanish (apparently over their apprehension about sharks).

"I think they had better learn to swim first," Maggie laughed.

Bethany smiled, but underneath her smile was a jumble of emotions. She felt like her eyes had been opened for the first time. These kids had so little, and yet they didn't ask for the moon and the stars. They asked to go to the ocean.

Or to see God's face, Bethany thought, still unable to shake the memory of the ragged little boy who had stood in the doorway. He had been in the back of her mind through the entire video show, and she prayed with all of her heart that somehow, someway, she would have the chance to see that little boy again.

four

Bouncing down the road from the orphanage in Miguel's taxi, Bethany was uncharacteristically quiet as she thought about everything that had transpired.

"I wish they all could find a real family," Holly said suddenly, voicing what most of them were thinking. "I wish I could take a bunch of them home with me."

"I would hate to live like that," Malia admitted, and Jenna nodded.

"It's just not fair," Monica added, glancing around. "They're little kids!"

"It is tragic," Maggie allowed. "But it is much, much better than the world they came from."

"I can't even comprehend where they are now," Bethany said.

"Most of us who have been raised in a safe, secure environment *can't*," Sarah said gently. Bethany could tell by the look on her face that she had been affected as much as the team — if not more.

As Miguel's taxi came to the crest of the hill, Maggie spoke to him in Spanish, and he pulled off the road and drove half a block down a rutted dirt road. Ahead was a large steel fence.

"Let's get out here for a minute. I want to show you something," Maggie said, opening the door to a trash-covered dirt road studded with tumbleweeds.

"See that on the other side of the fence?"

The teens peered through the fence. Past several miles of empty rolling hills they could see a busy freeway, homes, and businesses. In the far distance, skyscrapers thrust upwards like massive stalagmites.

"On the other side of this fence is the United States, and the city you see in the distance is San Diego," Maggie pointed out. "But on this side of the fence, life is much different."

Bethany and the team remained silent as they took it all in: the shacks, rough block homes, and half-completed houses that pushed up to the fence line. Litter, mangy stray dogs, and a dirty confusion of colors, smells, and noises assaulted them.

And yet, just a few miles away unimaginable wealth, beauty, order, and cleanliness sparkled in the hazy afternoon light.

"Do you ever wonder why?" Maggie asked suddenly. "Why you were born on that side instead of this side? Was it a gift? A mere accident or roll of the cosmic dice? A test ... or something else?"

Bethany felt a strange uncomfortable sensation come over her, like she had been eating food in front of someone who was starving. The team's silence spoke volumes, and she knew that they, like her, were searching their souls for answers to Maggie's questions.

Maggie walked around to face them, a gentle smile on her face. "Now that I've given you some tough stuff to think about, I feel I should take you for some genuine Tijuana tacos for dinner!"

"Yeah!" Dano called out from the back of the crowd. Kai elbowed him, and the team laughed a relieved kind of laugh.

"Are they safe to eat?" Monica asked warily.

"No worries," Maggie laughed. "Groups from our dormitory eat there all of the time."

"No magic punch?" Dano asked innocently.

"Magic punch?" Maggie and Sarah asked at the same time.

"Yeah," Dano grinned. "You drink it and then disappear into the bathrooms—like magic!"

Everyone groaned.

"You're so gross," Malia laughed.

"But entertaining," Kai added with a grin.

Miguel pulled the taxi up to the taco stand. The taco stand was crowded with the kids from the two vans. Many were filthy and covered with paint, mud, and cement. A number were talking excitedly about their day.

"You should have seen Matt try to pound a board in place!" One of the guys laughed. "He got one hit for every five swings of the hammer ... until finally they put him on paint duty!"

"I didn't bring my glasses," Matt pleaded to no avail as his friends continued to laugh.

Behind the counter, several workers cooked strips of beef on a charcoal barbecue. They chopped the cooked beef with lightning speed into small morsels that were scooped into a taco shell loaded with guacamole, onions, and a dash of make-you-sweat hot sauce.

The small tacos were cheap and delicious. Some of the guys had already plowed through half a dozen and were aiming at making it a full dozen.

"Bethany! You have got to try one of these— they're awesome!" Holly exclaimed before she took another huge bite of her taco.

"How do I do this?" Bethany asked Maggie.

"You order however many tacos you want as well as a soft drink or water, and enjoy—you don't pay until you are finished."

"Aren't they afraid that someone in a group this large will rip them off?"

"No, they know that this group is with us at the dorm," Maggie smiled. "They trust the word of Christians."

"Wow, that's cool!"

"That's how it should be," Maggie shrugged.

"Our word *should* be worth something," Sarah added.

Monica glanced over at Bethany with a shared look that said she'd overheard the conversation and remembered Bethany saying the same thing back at the dorm.

The worker behind the counter handed Bethany a plate with several tacos on it, and she hurriedly sank her teeth into one.

"Ohhh ... these are sooooo good!"

Holly grinned. "Told you so!"

"That was a great video of you surfing," Maggie said. "Was that all in one day?"

"Different days and different places," Bethany said, taking another bite of her taco. "Some of it is contest footage."

"Did you win the contest?"

"Some of them I win and some I don't," Bethany said.

"You missed it by an inch on the last one," Holly interjected.

"Yeah, it was one of those days that I couldn't seem to catch any waves," Bethany admitted. "But it worked out okay in the end. I wouldn't have been able to come here if I had won."

"How so?"

"Well, there's a big contest in Orange County right now that I would normally be seeded in."

"Seeded?"

"Get an instant spot in the finals," Monica supplied.

Bethany nodded. "But because I came in fifth place in my last contest, I wasn't able to be seeded in this contest. But that made me available for this trip instead."

"Do you have to be in contests?"

"Well, my sponsor likes for me to be in the contests," Bethany grinned. "And I like competing too."

"That's an understatement," Holly snorted. "She lives for a good challenge!"

Kai coughed into his napkin at the table as if to emphasize the point, and Maggie chuckled.

"A good challenge, huh? Well, I promise you won't go home disappointed, Bethany."

Bethany didn't ask Maggie what she meant by that. Instead, she took another bite of her taco and chewed slowly. She'd already come to the conclusion that today was just the tip of the iceberg.

After a five-minute sprinkling back at the dorm, which most of the girls didn't feel was even close to a long-enough shower, they settled in their bunks and began chatting about their day.

"Doesn't this place have central heating? It is freezing in here!" Monica exclaimed as she burrowed under the covers on her bunk.

"Zip yourself up in your sleeping bag and you'll be fine," Bethany said, sounding content from the depths of her own sleeping bag.

Holly, Malia, and Jenna quickly followed suit and were huddled in their bags just as the lights went out.

"At least we don't have to live in one of those tiny old shacks," a voice noted from somewhere in the room. "Can you imagine how cold they get?"

"I couldn't have imagined a lot of things I saw today—until I saw them," another voice said soberly.

"We went to an orphanage," Bethany said. "It was so sad to see all those little kids ... and no parents to love them."

"I never even knew this kind of world existed until I came here," Malia said.

"You mean you never saw the pictures of poor people on TV?" Holly asked.

"Yeah, I saw them ... but they were just pictures. It was never *real* to me."

Others agreed softly.

"I really admire Eddie and Maggie," Bethany said. "They don't have to work and live down here. They're Americans and could be living large across the border—instead they choose to spend their lives helping the poor. It really makes you think."

"It makes me appreciate what I've got," Monica admitted softly.

"It makes me feel stupid for complaining to my mom that I don't have enough clothes or that our house is so small," Jenna confessed.

"I had a doll house bigger than the house we built today," another girl said close to Bethany's bunk.

"What are we doing tomorrow? Does anyone know?"

"I know we don't have to worry about the van being stolen again. Sarah says Mike is sleeping in the new one tonight—just to be on the safe side."

"I heard that we were going to help give baths to kids," Holly said.

"Now that's a unique concept. Are they going to *want* these baths? I mean we're talking about little kids, right?" Bethany said grinning in the dark.

Holly giggled. "Oh, these kids will want them. Eddie said they don't have running water. He said that these kids only get a bath once every six weeks. So, there should be like a couple hundred kids lining up for a bath by the time we get there!"

"Oh, this is going to be fun," Bethany said, remembering the eager faces of the little boys at the orphanage.

"We also get to check kids for *ukus*—except they don't call them ukus here; they call them lice. Maggie said other groups that came from Hawaii were pros at finding them."

"Probably because every kid in Hawaii has had ukus at least once," Bethany said yawning.

"Yuck! *I've* never had them," Monica stated emphatically.

"Yeah, they wouldn't dare, huh, Monica?" Jenna teased, and the girls laughed.

"It just came to me who Monica and Jenna remind me of!" Bethany exclaimed. "Anyone ever see that movie *Grumpy Old Men*?" The girls burst out laughing again. "That's them—except they are grumpy young women."

"Grumpy young women *with* lice!" Holly added with flair.

"I'm starting to feel itchy. Can we talk about something else?"

The girls laughed—including Monica and Jenna. But the truth was Monica wasn't alone with how she felt; just talking about lice made everyone feel like scratching their heads like crazy.

The conversation slowed, and in the dark, the deep breathing of sleep could be heard mingling among the last whispered conversations of girls who had not yet given in to their exhaustion.

Bethany stared up at the dark ceiling, listening to the noise of traffic filtering in through the window. She thought once again about the little boy who wanted to see God's face.

The best father you could ever imagine having. In spite of the bitter cold that seeped through his thin blanket, Eduardo smiled as he thought about the words of the girl visiting the orphanage. His mother had told him God was the father in his dream. The girl had said it even better. Eduardo bit his lip. *It had to be true!*

He squeezed his eyes shut and prayed— prayed like he had never done before—and asked God to please let him see his face. His brothers, after all, remembered the man they called father— remembered what his face looked like. *I need a memory like they have,* Eduardo prayed fervently. *That way if I see you again, I'll know who you are—I'll know I have a father of my own that is watching out for me.*

five

"This morning all of you will have a chance to do something very simple and very humble," Eddie said as Bethany and the team gathered in the meeting area of the dorm after breakfast. "We are going to a place called The Dump to give the children who live there a chance to get a quick shower and shampoo and some clean clothes. These are children and families who make their living collecting salvageable materials from the dump. They have next to nothing.

"Now you can look at giving these poor dirty kids a bath as just a nice thing for one human being to do for another ... and you would be right. But maybe, just maybe, when you are doing it for one of these little ones—one of these overlooked and ignored kids—you can think that you are really doing it for Christ himself."

Eddie smiled at them and then glanced to where Sarah was standing.

"Now, before we head out, your youth director has a Scripture passage she would like to share with you."

Sarah, looking as fresh and pretty as ever with her blonde ponytail and perfectly applied makeup—something that didn't go unnoticed with Holly—quickly opened her Bible. "I know I've read this verse to you all before, but I just thought it might encourage us before we head out today. It's in Mathew 25:35–40.

"'For I was hungry and you gave me something to eat, I was thirsty and you gave me something to drink, I was a stranger and you invited me in, I needed clothes and you clothed me, I was sick and you looked after me, I was in prison and you came to visit me.'

"Then the righteous will answer him, 'Lord, when did we see you hungry and feed you, or thirsty and give you something to drink? When did we see you a stranger and invite you in, or needing clothes and clothe you? When did we see you sick or in prison and go to visit you?'

"The King will reply, 'I tell you the truth, whatever you did for one of the least of these brothers of mine, you did for me.'"

Sarah closed her Bible and looked around the room. "I guess Eddie couldn't have been more right about us doing this for God."

It was a short devotional, but so powerful, Bethany thought as a peaceful silence fell over the room. Even Kai and Dano, who often had a hard time settling down and focusing, appeared to have dialed right in on what Sarah was trying to say.

The caravan soon left the dorm and wormed its way back through the city, then veering off to take the bouncy, rock-strewn dirt roads.

Even though the vans' windows were shut tight against the dust, the dump broadcasted itself with its strong, pungent odor long before it was ever seen.

"Yuck! What's that smell?" Holly said, wrinkling her nose.

"The sweet smell of trash," Eddie grinned. "Rotting trash ... the aroma of a working landfill."

"I'm gonna gag!" Monica declared.

"Ah, don't be such a baby," Jenna said airily.

Bethany said nothing. She stared silently out the window at the broken skeletons of cars along the road, the tiny shacks that were dug into steep dusty hillsides, and the treeless, brown landscape. She thought of the little boy and the other children who had to face this every day, and she hoped like crazy that they could make some kind of difference.

As the caravan of vans pulled behind a trash truck and waited until it was clear to pass, Eddie began to tell them how he had discovered this mini-city in the bowels of the public dump.

"I had heard there were people living near the dump, but I didn't know where it was. I asked around and got lots of different answers because the dump tends to move locations. Once they have filled up a canyon with trash, they go find another canyon. So, finally it comes to me — kind of like God knocking on my forehead — if you want to find an active dump, try following a dump truck. I did, and it led me right to the dump and to the people who live near it."

The dump truck moved out, opening the way for the vans, and they continued on. The smell of the landfill strengthened. As the vans rounded the corner, the youth group from Hawaii could see dozens of dump trucks busily depositing their loads while tractors plowed the new refuse into the mountains of garbage. Overhead, what seemed to be thousands of seagulls glided above the piles of garbage like vultures, looking for a leftover that could become dinner.

"Look! There's something going on in the trash," Holly said, her face pressed against the window.

"There are *people* digging through the trash piles! They have bags around them," Monica said with a note of disbelief.

"Um, weren't you listening?" Jenna said. "These are the people Eddie's been telling us about."

The caravan of vans created a stir among the black dots digging through the trash. Suddenly a number of them — all small — streamed out of the trash piles toward the vans.

"They're kids!" Bethany said, finally finding her voice.

"I think you're right, Dorothy," Kai said as he stared somberly out the window.

Some of the children appeared to be as young as five or six. Their hands and arms were black with filth, their clothes were soiled beyond imagination, and their shoes were terribly worn and dark with scum. But their eyes beamed with brightness, Bethany noticed. And they laughed and chattered as if they were getting ready to attend a birthday party.

"I can't believe what I'm seeing," Dano said.

The vans pulled up next to a large concrete slab, which apparently had once been the foundation of a warehouse.

Today, Eddie informed them, it would be their bathhouse.

Another team, who had come over for the day from San Diego, had already erected an ingenious contraption made of PVC pipes and tarps that would serve to separate the makeshift rooms for the little boys and girls.

A team of leaders, many of them Mexicans who worked with Eddie's ministry, were guiding the process.

As Bethany got out of the van, she saw a collection of tiny buildings crammed together in the barren corner of the landfill. They seemed to be made of wooden pallets and roofed with blue tarp.

Bethany grabbed Eddie's arm as he walked by. "What are those?" she asked, pointing to the shacks.

"Those are the homes of the people who live and work in the dump," Eddie replied simply before moving on to help one of the teams.

Sure enough, erupting from the hovels were scores of small children, running as fast as their little legs could carry them. They were followed by women and a few teens.

The sight of immense poverty along with the nauseating smell of the dump threatened to over-whelm Bethany. For a brief moment she thought of retreating to the van. Then she reminded herself why she was there and quickly plunged into the crowd of filthy children who were as taken aback by her missing limb as she was by their grime.

Eddie called out to them in Spanish, and soon they were forming two lines: one for boys, the other for the girls. Meanwhile, Bethany and her team struggled to finish erecting the bathhouse. Others brought in sacks of clean used clothes, tow-els, detergent, and five-gallon jugs of hot water.

"How did they know we were coming?" Bethany asked Eddie as he handed her a stack of towels.

"I stopped by last week and told them we would be here today. They have come to trust our word."

"But what if it rained or something? The road to this place would be impossible to travel on."

"We would find a way," Eddie answered with a look of grim determination. "We promised them, and with people who don't have much hope in life, our promises mean everything."

Soon, tables were set up with piles of clothing. Just outside the bathhouse a station was erected for those found to be infested with lice. Plastic gloves and bottles of medicine designed to kill the creatures were laid out.

Inside the door of the bathhouse, a table held a huge stack of towels. Each towel had a Velcro strip sown into it. Bethany overheard Eddie tell Sarah that the towels were the work of love from a wheelchair-bound woman who had once come for a day visit. The woman had been so touched by the ministry of the bathhouse, she had decided she had to help. Buying and sewing the strips of Velcro on hundreds of towels had drained her small savings—not to mention her strength—but she felt it was only right to help preserve the modesty and dignity of the children.

Bethany couldn't help but think that maybe someday Jesus would thank this woman for providing him with a towel.

A small stool, a basin of water, and a bristle brush were placed at the entrance to each shower room.

"I need someone who is willing to wash feet!" Sarah called out.

A couple of the girls gave each other curious looks and then raised their hands. Several guys followed suit.

"After the kids change into a towel and put their dirty clothes in a bag, they will come here for a foot washing," Sarah instructed. "Make sure to use the scrubber. Some of these kids have feet that are thick with dirt."

The girls nodded.

"When their feet are clean, you can have them get in line for a shower. One of Eddie's staff will handle the rest."

The shower consisted of a large metal wash tub with a curtain on a circular plastic pipe base. The shower water came from a generator-powered pump placed in a five-gallon container of warm water.

The shower device was a simple sprayer, like one would find on a kitchen sink, controlled by a staff member who was experienced at rationing just enough water for each child.

Bethany couldn't help thinking that the five-minute showers they were allowed at the dorm would be a luxury here. And the long hot showers taken at home would be like going to heaven.

"See if you can sort these clothes out into piles of large, medium, and small," Sarah said, leading Bethany to the clothing table. "When a little girl comes to the table, let her pick out clothes that she thinks will fit and take her to the changing room. She will have her old clothes in a bag so make sure she goes home with them too."

Bethany blinked, trying to take in all that Sarah had quickly rattled off.

"And don't worry. We'll get you some help as soon as everything settles down a little. We have lots and lots of kids who need baths!"

As soon as the crew finished loading supplies into the makeshift bathhouses, kids started moving through the process as if it were a well-oiled machine.

Malia, who had pulled uku duty, carefully inspected the head of each girl for the small white eggs clinging to hair follicles that are the telltale sign of head lice. (She had pulled her own long hair up into a twist on top of her head ... just to be safe.)

Children who had lice were pulled out of line and taken to a table where their hair was washed with a powerful anti-lice shampoo. They were told to sit on a bench for fifteen minutes before being allowed back in line.

Inside the bathhouse, the foot-scrubbing girls were astonished at the amount of thick grime that worked its way into the feet of the children from standing in the refuse. None had socks, they told Bethany, and their shoes had been reduced to scraps.

Soon, the kids were coming through the line so quickly that Bethany did not have much chance to even try to talk to them. Occasionally she would ask a name, and every once in a while a small child would innocently point to the knotted sleeve of Bethany's arm and say something in Spanish. Bethany guessed it was a question about her arm.

Bethany would point to her missing arm and say "Tiburon" while watching the little eyes open in surprise.

Sometimes a child would come with a message from a worker printed in black felt pen on her hand. It might read: *Needs shoes,* which was a signal for Bethany that this particular girl's shoes were so bad that replacements needed to be found.

A large box of used children's shoes under the clothing table served as the shoe store.

"We have no socks!" Bethany called out when trying to find some to go with shoes she was giving to a little girl.

"We run out of socks quickly. People just don't donate them much," one of Eddie and Maggie's staff members called back to her. Bethany felt like crying.

"Okay, I guess you go sockless, young lady," she said softly to a pretty but uncomprehending girl of around seven.

"Your relief is here! Go take a break," Jenna announced as the little girl took off out the door with her new shoes.

Bethany went over the routine with Jenna and then stepped outside for a breath of fresh air—*as fresh as it could be at a dump*, she thought.

Just past the bathhouse, several girls from her group had set up an impromptu beauty salon and were busy painting the nails of giggling, happy little girls and combing out their thick black hair, which they decorated with ribbon and clips.

The roar of the trash trucks in the distance mixed with the squawking seagulls and the laughter and babbling of children. These sounds enveloped Bethany as she walked along, and she found herself smiling. She had done a lot of things in her fifteen years. Many of them seemed thrilling or important, but as she breathed in the tainted air and surveyed the makeshift bathhouse and the damp, happy children, she thought that just maybe what she had been a part of today was far more important then anything she had ever accomplished.

It felt right and good. And for the little child that no longer slept in filthy clothes, ate with blackened hands, or itched from ukus, she knew it made a difference—a real difference.

She just wished—

"Wanna see the 'town' Bethany?" Eddie asked, startling her from her thoughts.

Bethany bit her lip and looked behind her at the beehive of activity at the bathhouse.

"Don't worry," Eddie said with a smile. "There are plenty of workers today! A lot of the time we give baths with just our own workers. Come on, I'll show you around. Sarah said she wanted to come too."

Eddie signaled Sarah, and she joined the pair as they walked over the hard-packed road imbedded with trash.

Crowded together on the edge of the landfill were dozens of small shacks. Some had tin roofs; some had a mixture of tar paper and blue tarp.

A modest amount of electricity had been illicitly rigged from a nearby power line by a dangerous but ingenious system of extension cords.

"These people make their living by digging through the trash for aluminum cans, bottles, or anything they can sell," Eddie explained as they walked. "They follow the dump around. When this one fills up, they will all move to the new dump site."

"Why do the children work? Shouldn't they be in school?"

"Well, they should be in school, but it's complicated here. Going to school in Mexico involves some expenses, and these people can't afford much. In addition, the children are needed to help with the scavenging. Going to school would mean not enough money coming in to survive. It's a tough, cruel world here."

Eyes followed the trio as they slowly walked through the maze of shanties. Many times Eddie, who was loved and known in this slum, stopped to talk to someone along the way. Each time he stopped, Bethany had the strangest feeling someone was watching her.

"It seems news travels fast, Bethany. I've had to tell the short version of the shark attack three or four times now," Eddie laughed.

A small boy of about five darted between two homes and into their path, kicking the sad ragged remains of a soccer ball.

Bethany, who had played soccer seriously as a young girl, immediately jumped into action, deftly stealing the ball away from the little boy.

The boy laughed delightedly as he went after his ball. And it wasn't until he turned around that Bethany realized who he was.

"Eduardo!" she said happily, and he smiled and kicked the ball around her with the precision of a surgeon.

Bethany's soccer skills were somewhat rusty, and she did all she could to get and keep control of the ball. But every time she came in contact with the ball, the little scrapper joyously attacked as if he were in a national tournament.

Eddie watched the pair laughing and sparing along the dusty trash-strewn road.

"This kid is pretty good!" Bethany exclaimed with a shout to Eddie and Sarah.

Finally Eduardo stole the ball from Bethany and dribbled it to a hole in a pallet fence that served as his makeshift goal.

He grinned broadly as he kicked the ball in for a point.

"Little rascal," Bethany laughed.

Eddie waved the boy over and acted as interpreter for Bethany.

"He says he is five, and he lives here with his mother, four brothers, and a sister. He usually has to work in the dump, but his mother said he could have the day off—to stay clean. He likes to play football (which means soccer in Mexico) and wants to be on the national team someday," Eddie translated.

"Wow! Such ambition from such a young kid!" Sarah said, smiling down at the boy warmly.

"If he keeps playing like he did with me, he might make it," Bethany grinned.

Eduardo said something that caused Eddie to croak out, "*Como?*"

Eddie listened to Eduardo repeat what he said. Then Eddie translated for Bethany. "He says he heard you speak about God at the orphanage," Eddie said with a shake of his head. "He believes you will help him see the face of God."

"But I never said anything like—" Bethany felt Eduardo grab on to the edge of her sweatshirt.

"I think you have a fan," Sarah observed.

"I think I'm Eduardo's fan," Bethany replied, trying her best to blink back the tears that had formed in her eyes.

For the rest of the day, Bethany and Eduardo were inseparable. They played games of tag, played hopscotch in a course scratched out in the dirt, and ate snacks together from Bethany's backpack.

By mid-afternoon the last child had been bathed, and the team was busy dismantling the portable bathhouse and loading empty water containers into vehicles. Bethany strolled back to the slum with Eduardo and a few other children who had gathered around the tall blonde girl who was having so much fun with their friend.

As they walked, Eduardo grabbed Bethany's sleeve and pulled her toward one of the small houses with a blue tarp roof held in place by bricks and flat rocks.

"*Mi casa*," Eduardo said with a grin as he started pulling her toward the doorway.

Bethany wanted to stay outside the home, but Eduardo was having none of it.

As she stepped inside, she realized the home was even smaller than she had first imagined. It had only one window. Three sagging cots were pressed against the corner, and a small table with an old TV set was against the wall. Bethany noticed that the wires from the TV were connected to a car battery. A couple of beat-up chairs were wedged against the table, and next to it was a kerosene camp stove on a small stand with a few pots and pans underneath. The floor was merely layer upon layer of mismatched carpet laid on the bare ground.

A small, thick-waisted young woman, who Bethany took to be Eduardo's mother, was sitting on the edge of a cot when the pair entered, and she flushed with embarrassment. She ran to meet Bethany while saying something that sounded like a scold to the young boy.

Bethany, for her part, felt out of place standing there. She quickly introduced herself and then edged back toward the door.

She slipped outside and took a deep breath. It had only been a glimpse, but what she had seen shocked her more than anything she had witnessed in all of her travels.

Then the shock quickly melted into compassion as Eduardo appeared again with his pathetic-looking soccer ball in hand. He flashed a grin that persuaded Bethany to play another round with him.

They played on the plain of the dusty, seagull-infested landfill until Sarah called that they were getting ready to leave the site.

Bethany ran toward the caravan with Eduardo close at her heels. As the rest of her team wearily climbed into the vans, Bethany bent down and gave the boy a hug, trying to hold back the tears that threatened to spill down her cheeks as she told him good-bye.

Eduardo smiled, patted her cheek, and said something to her in Spanish.

"He says he knows he will see you again," Eddie translated with a sad smile that said that it wasn't likely to happen.

She glanced back at Eduardo, waved, and hurried into the van before the little boy could notice how upset she was—or see the lone tear that had escaped down her cheek. She would've given anything to stay a little longer—to feel like she had helped him more.

Bethany sniffed loudly as she plopped onto the seat next to Kai. "I think I'm getting a cold or something," she said, not looking at him.

"Must be catching," Kai whispered as he motioned to the seats behind them.

Bethany glanced back.

Holly, Malia, Jenna, and Monica were all sniffling as they looked out their windows at the mob of kids that congregated around the van. It was like the whole Hanalei girl's surf team had suddenly developed allergies ... to other's suffering.

An hour later, the grime of tramping around the dump with Eduardo had been scrubbed away, but the shower had done nothing about easing her troubled heart. Bethany sighed and sank down on one of the couches in the meeting room and waited for the other girls to finish their showers.

"Ready for another feast at the taco stand?" Eddie asked, rubbing his hands together as he entered the room.

Bethany shrugged. "I guess I don't have much of an appetite tonight." She sighed again. "Isn't there some way we can help those people out—I mean help them *more*?"

"You did more today than you realize," Maggie said with an understanding smile as she entered the room.

"Yeah, well it didn't feel like enough," Bethany said as Maggie sat down beside her.

"We are not going to end poverty," Eddie said soberly. "Even Jesus pointed out that 'the poor you will have with you always.' But we *can* make a difference—one person at a time."

"Have you ever heard the story of the starfish?" Maggie asked.

Bethany shook her head no.

Maggie smiled. "Imagine a huge tide coming in, washing up thousands of starfish all along the beach. When the tide goes out, thousands of starfish are left stranded. We all know what will happen once the sun comes up, right?"

"They'll dry up and die," Bethany replied slowly, trying to figure out where Maggie was going with the story.

"So, this man decides to take a stroll on the beach and is startled to find thousands of starfish lying about everywhere. Then he notices a young boy picking them up one by one and hurling them with all his might back into the ocean.

"The man watches the boy for a short time before he finally decides to approach him, saying, 'Son, you might as well give up. It's no use. There are just too many starfish. What you are trying to do makes no difference.'

"The young boy, holding a starfish in his hand, looks up at the man and then flings the starfish out into the water and says, 'Well, it made a difference to that one!' "

Bethany grinned for the first time in hours.

"We can't change the problems of the whole world," Eddie said gently, "but we can help change someone's world. If tonight a child goes to bed without hunger, without the itch of bugs, or with clean clothes, we have done something worthwhile."

"Can I see Eduardo again?" Bethany asked suddenly.

Eddie frowned. "We aren't scheduled to go back to the homes at the dump again for another month."

"My heart is telling me to buy Eduardo a new soccer ball—just something to let him know I believe in him," Bethany said shyly. When she looked up, she saw Eddie and Maggie looking at each other.

"Well . . . ," Eddie said with a slow smile spreading across his face. "Maybe we could swing by for a minute or two tomorrow."

"Really? Thank you so much!" Bethany said excitedly. Then she thought for a moment and added, "Uh, can you tell me where I can buy a soccer ball around here?"

Eddie and Maggie smiled and hugged Bethany.

"How about this: after dinner, Maggie and I will take all of you to downtown Tijuana. You can buy a soccer ball at Woolworth's . . . and watch everyone get suckered by the guys selling tourist stuff."

"Cool!" Bethany laughed.

After a hearty meal at the taco stand, the caravan wove through the packed streets of the tourist zone. As soon as they were parked, Sarah called them together.

"Listen up, guys, Eddie has some ground rules before you take off!"

"You have two hours to shop around. Remember, in this zone the first price is never the *real* price—unless you are a sucker." Everyone laughed and Eddie grinned. "Bargaining is part of the game here.

"Also, it's going to be impossible to keep track of all of you in the maze of shops and alleyways, so here is the deal: be back here in two hours. I will give you five minutes of grace time, and then we're leaving. If you're late, you'll just have to take a taxi back to the dorm." He then gave each student a business card with the address in Spanish.

"That's hard-core," Holly whispered to Bethany. "Do you think he would actually leave us here?"

"Aw, I don't *think* so . . . ," Bethany said, chewing on her lip thoughtfully. "But we better watch the time just in case."

The teens swarmed into the dens of the vendors selling everything from sombreros to Mexican jumping beans, while Bethany dragged Holly, Malia, Jenna, and Monica with her to buy Eduardo's soccer ball.

"They won't bargain for things in a department store," Monica lamented.

"Has that ever stopped you before?" Jenna asked, and Monica stuck her tongue out at her.

"Don't worry, Monica, you'll have your chance," Bethany laughed. And true to her word they were back outside in a flash, plunging into the neighboring small shops and kiosks with all of the wide-eyed wonder of tourists.

"Hey, pretty girls, come on inside. I got what you need; take a look!" shouted one of the vendors as they walked by.

"Cheaper than Kmart!" shouted another.

"What about Wal-Mart?" Bethany whispered, and Holly laughed.

Most shops had similar wares: blankets, T-shirts, black velvet paintings, piñatas, jewelry, and colorful serapes.

The girls quickly got into "buy mode," and each gave bargaining a try. It soon became apparent that Holly was the hardened deal-maker of the bunch, so each girl—when she saw something she thought she might be interested in—went to Holly and asked her to do the honors of bargaining for it.

Standing off to the side, they giggled to each other as Holly went through the motions of walking away from a price she thought was too high, only to have the shop vendor plead her back with another offer.

Soon their arms were loaded down. Monica, the whirlwind shopper of the bunch, held stacks of brightly patterned blankets, peasant tops, and skirts. Jenna had a tooled leather purse, and Malia bought a stuffed aardvark for her seventh-grade brother. Holly, true to her calling, had scored some lipstick and perfume—cheaper than Wal-Mart.

Bethany normally would've been right in the thick of it all, but instead she played the role of lookout for new bargains as she clutched the soccer ball tightly and merely looked. She didn't have the stomach for spending money on things she didn't truly need after today's brush with poverty.

The group walked farther and farther into the arcade of shops, chuckling as they were dragged into one after another by eager vendors.

"Uh, Holly, I hope you've been keeping track of the time," Bethany said as they stepped out of yet another shop.

"Oh, my gosh!" Holly exclaimed, glancing at her watch. "We've got to head back ... *now!*"

The girls burst into action, quickly weaving in and out of concession stands, crowded passage-ways, and kiosks.

"Are we lost?" Monica asked, sounding near hysteria. "Don't tell me we're lost! Oh, I DO NOT want to be lost in downtown Tijuana! Do any of you know where we are?"

"Relax," Bethany grinned. "I've been keeping an eye out. We should pop out on the main drag right past this next shop."

Sure enough, the girls turned the corner and found themselves once again on the noisy, tourist-packed Revolution Boulevard.

"See? Plenty of time to spare!" Bethany said as the girls made their way past photo-op carts with their donkeys painted to look like zebras toward the crowd that had begun to gather around the vans.

Kai and Dano looked like they were going to pass out from excitement.

"Look what I got!" Kai whispered urgently as he walked up to Bethany.

"What?"

Kai glanced over his shoulder. Dano did the same, and Bethany rolled her eyes.

"It's a Rolex—fully waterproof!" Kai said pulling back the sleeve of his sweatshirt to display a shiny gold watch. "Do you have any idea how much these cost in the States? And I got it for thirty bucks!"

"A real Rolex?" Bethany asked, suddenly smelling a rat.

"It says Rolex, doesn't it?" Kai glanced at Dano with a "girls—what do they know?" look.

Then Jeff, one of the North Shore body board crew, strolled up and crowed about the great deal he got on a new watch.

Jeff held out his arm and showed off the identical watch that Kai had just purchased. "Ten bucks! Can you believe it? Ten bucks for a Rolex!"

Bethany bit her lip to keep from laughing. The look on Kai's face was payment enough—or so she thought—until Eddie arrived.

"Oh, I see you bought yourself a Rolex," he said with a grin as he spotted the watches on the boys' wrists. "I hear they're guaranteed to run at least up to the border," he said, suppressing a laugh.

"Whatd'ya mean?" Kai asked, looking between Eddie, Sarah, and Maggie. "Aren't they real?"

"Real fakes," Eddie laughed again.

"But they say Rolex," Kai argued.

"Made by Rip-Off," Eddie quipped.

Kai groaned, and everyone laughed.

"Don't worry, Toto, we'll be back in Kansas before you know it," Bethany grinned as she climbed into the van.

"Gee thanks, Dorothy," Kai muttered somewhere behind her.

Bethany laughed as she sank into her seat and gazed down at the soccer ball she had bought. She felt as if she were the happiest shopper in the whole van.

six

Eduardo crawled out of bed and blinked a couple of times as he looked around the room. He could have sworn that he heard someone calling his name, but his mother and older brothers and baby sister were already gone. Shivering, he padded across the room to see if there was any food left over from the night before. He found a tablespoon of refried beans left in the pan. Eduardo grabbed up a tortilla from the shelf below and hurriedly scooped the beans into his mouth.

His family would already be on their way to work through the huge pile of trash that was forming from the morning's first delivery. His brothers had told him that his friend Bethany must have worked very hard to surf again after the tiburon had taken her arm. His mother agreed. God liked to see people work hard at their jobs, she'd told him, so that was just what he was going to do.

Maybe if he worked hard enough, God would let him see his face.

Eduardo slipped on his dirty shoes and went to join them.

Bethany picked at her breakfast as Sarah finished telling them all about the change of plans for the day.

She felt a little guilty about her lack of enthusiasm—especially since the change had been brought about because of her—but she was worried.

"This is very unusual for the orphanage to make such a request on behalf of the children," Eddie said with a pleased smile. "They tend to be very, very protective of their children—especially with none of them being able to swim. The only reason they are letting the kids visit the ocean today is because your group made such a good impression on them."

"Your presentation really inspired those boys," Maggie added with a wink at Bethany.

Bethany nodded and managed to smile but continued to worry on the inside. She had felt so strongly about giving little Eduardo that soccer ball. What if things kept cropping up and she never made it back to him before she had to go home?

"Bethany?" Eddie said, suddenly startling her from her thoughts. "You might want to bring the soccer ball with you."

"Really?" she said, trying not to sound too desperately hopeful. Kai heard it in her voice, though. He shot her a supportive grin from across the table.

"I gave you my word that I would take you. What kind of Christians would we be if we didn't keep our word?"

Bethany nodded again — this time happily. Then she caught Monica staring at her thoughtfully, like she was trying to figure something out.

Bethany didn't mind. She was too busy thinking about the little boy with the dream of becoming a soccer player ... and a smile that could melt an iceberg.

Eduardo wandered over the crushed wasteland toward the rubbish pile where his family was working. Trash trucks rolled by, their hydraulic lifts hissing as raw refuse and bags of trash hit the ground.

Eduardo watched a small group rush forward to rip into the rotting and stinking trash bags to search for bottles, cans, or bits of metal.

Most people carried a gunnysack type bag into which they threw any recyclable materials they found. When a bag became too heavy to drag along, the worker would take the full bag back to the family's home. There the bag was emptied into a pile to be separated later.

The job of sorting out the various materials was done by the youngest children in each family. The child sorted the materials into large piles of glass bottles, tin cans, and other bits of aluminum. These materials accumulated until they could be sold by weight. This summer, at the age of five, Eduardo had graduated from sorting to searching for materials.

"Eduardo, *trabajo!* (*work!*)," his older brother shouted over the noise. Eduardo quickly picked up a greasy blackened bag.

Using a stick, he poked a hole into the bag of trash. Then he rifled through the contents with his hands, holding his breath for as long as he could against the horrid odor.

He was rewarded with four or five beer bottles, several soda cans, and half a dozen tin cans. He dropped them into his sack and poked his stick into another bag.

This time it was a jackpot! The bag was literally full of cans and bottles. *Maybe this is leftover from a party or something,* he thought excitedly as bag after bag yielded similar results. He filled his sack until it was difficult for him to drag it along, let alone lift. But all Eduardo could think of was how proud his mother would be with his discovery— how proud God would be!

Huge garbage trucks continued to sweep into the area. They backed up quickly to deposit their loads and then drove off again.

Eduardo struggled with his overstuffed sack as it became snagged repeatedly on broken pieces of refuse or bits of rubble.

The crashing and grinding sound of the garbage trucks was all around Eduardo as he gritted his teeth and pulled for all he was worth.

Suddenly he saw the giant shadow of a truck loom over him. Its massive double wheels backed up over his precious sack of treasure.

Eduardo yelled as he struggled to free his gunny sack. The roar of rolling trash filled his ears as the contents of the truck crashed around him.

The truck's airbrakes sounded, and the wheels turned and released the sack Eduardo was tugging on. As the bag broke free, Eduardo tumbled on his back into a tangled mass of rubbish ... and before he could react, the black double wheel of the garbage truck came rolling down on him.

When the Hawaiian youth group got to the orphanage, the children were almost beyond themselves with excitement. They chatted nonstop and bounced up and down with energy that Holly noted would put Bethany to shame.

"I say we join them," Bethany said, feeling better about the day knowing that she would be able to see Eduardo as well. Holly looked at her like she had lost her mind but followed her into the raggedy old van that belonged to the orphanage. The kids squealed in delight.

"When am I ever going to learn to just say no?" Holly said as she smiled at Bethany and let herself get pulled into a seat with an excited group of boys.

"Sorry to have to break it to you, but I don't think that's going to happen," Bethany said as one of the little boys wrapped his arms around her neck. "So, you might as well just sit back and enjoy the ride!"

Soon the ocean's blue horizon came into view, and the vans parked on a small dirt cliff just above the beach. The van doors opened, and a wave of children quickly scrambled down a tiny trail to the white sand below. The teens and adults had to work hard to keep up with them and prevent them from running straight into the ocean.

As Bethany ran with the children to the beach, her eyes quickly went to the surf crashing on the shore. *Looks like this place has some surfing potential after all,* she thought just as she spotted a perfectly shaped "left" racing in.

"Oh, my gosh!" Bethany exclaimed, nudging Holly, "Did you see that wave?"

"Yeah, too bad you don't have a surfboard or bathing suit," Holly sympathized.

"I *do* have a bathing suit. I am wearing it under my clothes," Bethany grinned. "When I heard we were coming to the beach, I ran upstairs and put it on."

"I wish I would've thought of that," said Holly.

"Okay, we gotta quit eyeballing the surf and go play with the kids," Bethany said. She shook herself from the wave-induced trance long enough to remember what they were there for.

Holly grinned. "Thanks for bringing me back to earth."

"Yeah, well, I needed to hear it too," said Bethany.

"What you *need*," Kai said, startling them as he ran by with a giggling little boy in his arms, "is to show these kids how we have fun at home, Dorothy!"

"Wait up, Toto!" Dano called as he ran by, his little passenger riding on his shoulders.

"Hey, that's my line," Bethany yelled as she and Holly raced after them.

For the next hour, Bethany and her friends chased the small fries around the sand, splashed in the shoreline, and made sand castles.

Lunch was brought down, and Bethany washed the sand off her hands in the tiny incoming waves. She shivered in the icy water as she waded in up to her calves.

As the group sat on the sand eating their lunch, a car pulled up on the bluff. Out poured three blond-headed surfers. Bethany noticed one pointing excitedly to the "left" she had seen earlier in the day. Before long, the young men clad in wet suits were trudging down the cliff with surfboards under their arms.

"Look, surfers," Bethany said to the little boy sitting next to her. She pointed to the young men paddling out through the white water.

The little boys leaned forward in rapt attention. Every eye was fixed on the surfers' performance, and each time one of them took a wipeout, the children laughed delightedly.

Bethany smiled, thinking the guys surfing that afternoon might never again have such an appreciative audience as they had that day.

"*Tu* surf?" one of the children asked, suddenly turning back to Bethany.

"He is asking if you are going surfing," Eddie supplied with a smile.

"I figured," Bethany said, chewing on her lip thoughtfully. "No, no *tabla*." Bethany shrugged her shoulders. "Eddie, is that the right word for surfboard?"

"Yeah, you've got it."

"Ah!" the boy nodded, but she didn't miss the disappointment on his face.

Soon the young surfers began to drift in and walk up the cliff to their car. Bethany saw that they noticed with curiosity the mix of dark-skinned little boys and American teens. When she turned back around, she also noticed that Holly was gone.

The next thing Bethany knew, Holly was standing in front of her with a surfboard in her arms.

"The guys said you could borrow this. They know who you are and would be pretty excited to see you surf," Holly said with her trademark Cheshire-cat grin. Then she added, "Sarah and Eddie already said it was okay."

Bethany shook her head at Holly and then took the board from her hands. "I am going to freeze my butt off without a wet suit," she whispered.

"Good thing," Holly replied breezily. "That way you won't stay out too long."

Eddie announced to the children that Bethany would be showing them how she surfed. Moments later, Bethany was slowly plowing her way into the surf.

Bethany was shivering in the icy water and wondering if she could handle the cold. But then she remembered stories of how her mom "trunked" it through winters in San Diego and how her dad, wearing an antique, stiff wet suit had plodded through the snows of New Jersey to surf in the winter.

Don't be a baby; this is in your blood, she reminded herself. But she was still so cold her teeth chattered.

Okay then, think about the kids.

It didn't take Bethany long in the lineup to pick off her first wave. She paddled the unfamiliar surfboard as if she had ridden it her whole life and dropped into the medium-sized wave with grace and ease, stalling at just the right spot to get a short cover-up before rocketing to the end of the section.

The guys on the cliff stared in astonishment.

Bethany surfed on five or six waves before coasting to the beach. All of the children ran to meet her as she lifted herself out of the surf. Even the American guys on the cliff came down to talk to her.

"I have no idea *how* you did that!" one of them said.

"Can you believe that!" they said to each other, "I dare you to try to surf with one arm!"

Bethany smiled shyly and handed back the surfboard. "Thanks a lot you guys—you made their day," she said as the orphans jumped up and down around her like tiny pogo sticks.

"You made our day too," Kai said with a grin as he handed her a towel to wrap around her shoulders.

"I am soooo cold that if I had a stick in my mouth, you could sell me as a Popsicle," Bethany said in a shivery voice, and they all laughed.

With the show over and with pockets full of seashells, the orphans were herded back to the waiting vans.

As soon as she started to thaw, Bethany's thoughts immediately returned to Eduardo.

"Eddie, are we anywhere near the dump?"

"Did you bring the soccer ball?"

"Yeah," Bethany smiled. "In fact I hid it in the van so these kids wouldn't get it dirty. I want it to be nice, clean, and unused when I give it to Eduardo."

"You know, that may be the first new gift he has ever been given," said Eddie.

"Wow!" said Bethany.

"I think we can make a detour after we drop off these kids. Just one van though—we will send the rest back to the dorm to clean up for dinner."

"Thanks, Eddie, I appreciate it."

"Payment for freezing on our behalf today."

"Sounds like a fair trade," Bethany grinned.

As soon as they dropped the exhausted but grateful little group off at the orphanage, the group split up. The rest of the team headed for the dorm, while Eddie and Bethany made their way back to the dump.

Bethany looked for familiar markers as Eddie guided Mike, the driver, through the dusty and dirty roads. Soon enough, she was hit with the familiar smell of rotting garbage. And then the seagulls circling in the sky gave away the dump's location.

The single van bouncing down the rough road did not attract nearly as much attention as the caravan had on the previous day. Eddie directed the driver past the concrete slab that had been the home of the portable bathhouse and straight toward the squat collection of shacks.

Bethany reached behind the backseat of the van and grabbed the soccer ball. When the van came to a stop, she and Eddie hopped out.

"Thanks again for doing this, Eddie."

"I'm happy to do it. Do you remember where he lives?"

"Yeah, I remember," said Bethany as they picked their way past the homes made of pallets and tar paper.

"Here," she said, pointing excitedly to the low tarp-covered home.

Eddie knocked on the door but there was no response.

He tried again, calling out something in Spanish.

Again, no response.

Then a neighbor came outside and began to speak to Eddie in a quiet tone. Eddie suddenly became very animated ... and grim. While she wasn't sure what was being said, Bethany felt like something cold had dropped into the pit of her stomach.

Please, please don't let it be something bad, Bethany prayed earnestly.

"*Gracias, gracias,*" Eddie said to the neighbor, and then he turned to Bethany. "There's been an accident. Their neighbor said that Eduardo was run over by a trash truck this morning. They have taken him to the hospital. She says it is very bad, but other than that, she knows nothing."

Bethany felt herself begin to shake. This wasn't bad—it was horrible!

"Where? What hospital?" she cried.

"I don't know," Eddie replied gently. "Apparently the dump truck driver took them. I will find out, but first we need to go back to the dorm."

"Eddie, promise me that you will help me go see him in the hospital," Bethany pleaded.

Normally, Eddie would have politely dodged this request, but as he looked in Bethany's eyes, he saw them well up in tears, and something inside of him told him to agree.

"Yeah, okay, I promise."

"You won't change your mind?"

"Bethany, one thing you should know about me is that my yes is yes, and my no is no. If I make you a promise, I will keep it," Eddie replied carefully.

Bethany exhaled and nodded. "All right. Thank you."

The pair walked slowly back to the van. Bethany slipped the still unused soccer ball under her sweatshirt so that she could free her hand and dab the tears away from her eyes.

Back at the dorm, the teams formed an impromptu prayer meeting to pray for Eduardo. The atmosphere was solemn and quiet as they waited for Eddie to come back from his office where he was calling all of the hospitals in town, trying to get information about a boy who he only knew by his first name.

At the end of the prayer time, Eddie was back in the room.

"I found him," he said. "He's alive, but in bad shape. They say he might loose his leg. The family has no money, but I told them that if money was the issue, we would find it."

Suddenly the teenagers began digging in their pockets for money. Bethany fished out almost all she had and placed it in Eddie's hands.

The unexpected show of love and generosity caused Eddie to tear up.

"I guess we better head over to the hospital," Eddie said, glancing at Bethany.

"Just let me get something from my room," Bethany said. She was taking the stairs two at a time before anyone had the chance to reply.

seven

Anne Nicholson could rip. The young California surfer had jumped into the water in fourth grade, and by seventh grade she was blowing minds at her home break in Ventura, California.

Several years older than Bethany, Anne was at the end of her amateur career and about to step into the grueling world of professional women's surfing.

Already her pictures had appeared in surfing magazines, and she had an impressive array of sponsors. And it helped that her spunky, California-surfer-girl good looks made her great media material in ads and interviews.

She had surfed against Bethany before and admired her competitor's grit, determination, and skill.

When the waves were pumping, the two were neck in neck. But Anne knew that she had a slight advantage in places where the waves were small and mushy. And the last time Bethany and Anne had met in competition, the conditions favored Anne, not Bethany.

In Bethany's final regional contest, the two-foot, soft, crumbly waves had put Bethany slightly behind Anne in the running for the nationals. That is why Anne was at Trestles preparing for the nationals, and Bethany was in Tijuana.

Anne studied the swell before her with a grin. She was excited about the contest the following day. She entered the water at a break called the Rivermouth. Her first three waves were short close-outs, but she milked the most out of them, pulling into unmakable barrels or floaters over the collapsing white water.

The fourth wave looked similar to the previous three, but then Anne thought that there might be a possibility for an even deeper tube ride, and she stalled for a moment at the top of the wave.

It was a crucial error; before she could get the board to slip back down the face of the wave, the whole curl sucked over.

Anne found herself air-dropping out of control over the lip.

It happened in an instant.

The nose of her board dug into the base of the wave and flipped over as she followed it. Her body crashed onto the deck, as the weight of the wave collapsed onto her back. She felt the board sliding under her and instinctively covered her head with her arms to protect herself.

A sharp pain sliced through her leg as she impacted with the fins of her board. The whole wipeout was short in duration. As Anne put her feet on the sandy bottom and lifted her head out of the water, she could see her surfboard in two pieces and feel a growing pain coming from her thigh.

She limped onto the beach and noticed that her wet suit had a knife slice opening above her right knee, and blood was already starting to ooze.

The weakness in her leg told Anne that she had messed something up good, so without taking off her wet suit, she hobbled to her car and painfully drove herself to the emergency room.

It was early evening in Hawaii when the phone in the Hamilton home began to ring, but no one was there to answer it.

Several hours later, Noah rolled in from a surf session and noticed that a message light was blinking on the phone.

It was Bethany's sponsor with some exciting news: Bethany was in the finals!

Anne's accident, while not career threatening, had sidelined her for the next few weeks. She would not be surfing tomorrow; the slot was open to the next highest contender, who happened to be Bethany.

Noah was excited for his sister. He knew her disappointment at not making it into the final contest of the year. He also knew she would drop anything and race to Orange County for the showdown.

But where in Mexico was Bethany and how could he get in contact with her? He would have to wait until his parents returned home to find that out.

Eddie roared through the thick Tijuana traffic, trying to get them to the hospital—to Eduardo as quickly as he could. Before tonight, Bethany had never paid much attention to the driving skills it took to maneuver around the massive roundabouts and crazy drivers for whom a stop sign was merely a suggestion. She glanced at Eddie. He seemed calm enough, but she noticed he drove with one hand on the wheel and the other on the horn.

The hospital was tucked away in an industrial area, and, unlike the hospitals Bethany had seen before, it was small and unimpressive.

Before leaving the car, Bethany grabbed the soccer ball she had bought for Eduardo.

The pair entered the foyer, and Eddie conversed with the nurse on duty who directed them to a waiting room.

Eddie paced around for a while and then stopped in his tracks. "Bethany, stay here. I want to talk to the administrators for a minute."

"Okay," she said, her eyes following Eddie until he faded out of sight.

Bethany turned and scanned the waiting room.

Other than an elderly woman, she was alone. She sighed and sat down on a hard plastic chair.

She looked around. The walls were blank. No pictures, no murals, and no signs in *any* language.

A small side table held dog-eared magazines that were obviously about celebrities but were written in Spanish.

Bored and anxious, Bethany stood and paced around the blank room, while random and disconnected thoughts and short prayers mingled and raced through her mind.

It was nearly twenty minutes later when Eddie returned.

"They are going to let us see him," he said. "I told the hospital people that we could get the money to pay for his surgery. They said his mother is with him. I don't know if there is a father in the picture or not. From what they say, it sounds pretty serious."

"How did it happen?"

"I don't really know. An accident of some kind. It's pretty dangerous in the dump with all those big rigs going back and forth and kids darting in and out of the trash. My guess is that the driver didn't see Eduardo."

"Won't the city take care of the medical costs? After all, it was one of their trucks that ran him over!"

Eddie smiled softly. "Those families are not supposed to be working or living at the landfill, Bethany. The officials just look the other way because there are no other real opportunities for them."

"What would happen to him if you didn't offer to pay the bill?"

"They would patch him up a little and send him home. If the wound was badly infected, he might die. Or he might live and be crippled for life. You would see him begging on the street corner in a few years."

"That's terrible!"

"That's reality," Eddie countered.

The idea that a little boy could be allowed to suffer because of a lack of money was just sinking into Bethany's head when a nurse came into the waiting room and spoke to Eddie.

"We can see Eduardo now," Eddie told her.

Bethany picked up the soccer ball and followed him down a narrow corridor to a small room where several beds lay.

Eduardo looked painfully tiny on the white-sheeted bed. His eyes were closed, and his leg was swathed in bandages. Next to him on a small vinyl chair was the same woman Bethany had met the day before. Lines of worry creased her face, but she stood as Eddie and Bethany came into the room. She rushed over to Eddie, taking his hands in hers as she sobbed out the story, occasionally gesturing toward her son.

Bethany inched closer to the bed, staring down at Eduardo as she tried to think of something she could say to him.

The boy stirred and opened his eyes.

"I have a gift for you," Bethany said softly, trying not to cry as she held up the soccer ball for him to see.

A smile beamed across the boy's face, and Bethany placed the ball in his arms. He shut his eyes again but kept a firm grip on the ball. A female doctor entered the room then and signaled to Eduardo's mother. Eddie politely asked if he could come along, and the doctor nodded yes.

Bethany took the empty seat next to Eduardo and prayed for the little boy.

A few moments later Eduardo's mother and Eddie returned. The woman's eyes were wet with tears.

Bethany quickly surrendered the chair, and Eddie pulled her off to one side.

"They are going to take his foot," Eddie whispered.

"What?" Bethany said, incredulous.

"Apparently, it is too crushed to save."

Bethany shook her head, unwilling to accept that kind of fate for Eduardo. He was only five years old! "We could take him to America. I bet they could save his foot there. We have experts for that kind of thing!" Bethany said loudly.

"Settle down," Eddie urged quietly. "You need to understand that there are limits to what we, and even you, are able to do. If the boy had connections or lots of money there'd be a chance that we could get him in front of doctors who could save his foot. But he doesn't. Even so, these doctors are going to do the best they can."

Bethany understood—even though she didn't want to. She felt drained of every ounce of energy she had ever had as she leaned against the wall.

"When?"

"First thing in the morning," Eddie answered grimly.

"Does he know?"

"No, they have him pretty sedated. They won't be telling him."

"I want to be here when he wakes up," Bethany said, suddenly determined not to take no for an answer. "Can you bring me back here tomorrow so I can be here when he wakes up?"

"Uh, yeah, sure," Eddie said, caught off guard by her tone.

"No, I need you to promise me that you will bring me here. It's important that somebody who has been through ... it's important that I be here when he wakes up," she said. Bethany saw understanding fill Eddie's eyes.

"You have my word on it."

Bethany turned and walked back to Eduardo's bedside. She knelt next to the boy and lightly touched his thick black hair.

"I will be here tomorrow when you wake up," she said softly. Then she turned back to Eddie. "Please tell him that I will be here tomorrow when he wakes up from his operation. Tell him it's a promise."

"I'll tell him. I'm not sure that he will remember. They have him pretty drugged up right now."

Eddie whispered to Eduardo, and Bethany heard her name mentioned.

The boy squeezed his soccer ball at the message.

"He understands," Bethany said, no longer able to stop the flow of tears from running down her cheeks. "He understands."

Cheri Hamilton came through the door with an armload of groceries and was almost mowed over by Noah as he grabbed the bags from her. "Where have you been? I have been trying to call your cell phone for over an hour!"

"I was grocery shopping. I forgot to charge my cell phone, so the thing died. Why? What's up?"

"Bethany is in the finals. One of the girls had to drop out, so Bethany is seeded into the contest tomorrow. But she doesn't know about it. Can you get ahold of her? Her sponsors have offered to pick her up in Tijuana and drive her to the contest. It's only an hour or so away."

"This is wonderful!" Cheri exclaimed. "She is going to be so excited! It was really hard on her to miss being in the finals by one slot."

"Not only that, but I've been on the computer checking the wave predictions for California, and it looks like they're going to have terrific conditions tomorrow."

"Wouldn't that be a great way to end the year—to win in the finals! Okay, we've got to find her," Cheri said as she began to shuffle through a pile of papers by the phone. "I have a list of contact numbers somewhere around here . . ."

Bethany and Eddie pulled into the dorm parking lot. The night air was cold. It cut through Bethany's sweatshirt when she got out of the car. For the first time that evening she remembered that she hadn't eaten.

"I'm gonna go fix myself a peanut butter and jelly sandwich. Do you want me to make you one too Eddie?"

"Sure," Eddie smiled. "In all the excitement I guess we forgot about dinner. If you don't mind, wrap it in a paper towel and I'll eat it on my way home."

"You bet!" Bethany said and headed straight for the kitchen.

As Eddie entered the dorm, he could hear the phone ringing in his office. No sooner than he began fumbling for the right key to unlock the door, the ringing stopped.

Eddie frowned.

Suddenly the phone started ringing again, and Eddie, who was prepared with key in hand, picked it up by the third ring.

"Bethany! You have a call from Hawaii," Eddie shouted down the hall.

Bethany stuck her head around the corner and said, "For me?"

"Yep!" said Eddie. "And time is ticking away 'cause it is long, long distance."

Bethany barreled down the hall, her lips sticky with peanut butter and jelly. She quickly dropped two sandwiches wrapped in a paper towel into Eddie's hand and grabbed the phone.

"Hi, Mom! What? The finals ... you're kidding? How? Is she okay? When? Tomorrow morning ... Trestles ... hold on."

Bethany cupped her hand over the phone. "I got in the finals, Eddie! A girl had to drop out, and I was next in line! They want to come and pick me up early in the morning at the race track. Do you know where that is?"

"Yep," Eddie said and then cleared his throat. "It's over where we were tonight—over by the hospital."

At those words, Bethany's face registered shock. How could she have forgotten Eduardo so soon?

"Mom, can I call you back in a little while? ... Okay.... Thanks, Mom."

Bethany sank into Eddie's office chair.

"I think I'm gonna stay a while and eat these sandwiches in the kitchen," Eddie said. "You're welcome to hang out in my office if you think you might need to use the phone again."

"Thanks," Bethany said weakly.

What am I gonna do?

There was no response—not even a whisper of help. Bethany felt as if her brain had turned to mush.

The long day and the crisis with Eduardo sapped her energy and emotions. Now with the news that she was suddenly to be seeded into the final—which should have been a moment of sheer joy—she was completely confused.

She dragged herself upstairs to the dorm room and was surprised to see the dorm lights blazing.

"We had a prayer time for Eduardo, and we've been sitting around talking," Malia said. "How is he?"

"It's bad. They are probably going to have to amputate his foot."

"Oh, no!" Holly said amid the others' audible gasps. "How did that happen?"

"He got run over by a trash truck while he was collecting trash," Bethany said sadly. "I guess his foot was almost severed or something. I couldn't understand exactly."

"Maybe they can get him to a specialist!" Monica offered.

"Yeah, I suggested that, but I guess it's not that easy when you're a dump kid from Tijuana."

The group fell silent for a moment, weighing the gulf between their lives and Eduardo's.

"And, I just found out that Anne Nicholson had to pull out of the contest tomorrow, so now I can surf in the finals. My mom called from home."

"Wow! That's terrific!" Jenna said.

"What happened to Anne?" Holly asked.

"She banged herself up at Rivermouth. Not too serious, but she will be out of the water for a couple of weeks."

"When is the contest?"

"Heats start tomorrow," said Bethany.

"How would you get there?" asked Holly.

"My Rip Curl rep said he would drive down here and pick me up in the morning. We could make it for the girls' division heat since it's at Trestles."

"Bethany, you are sooooo lucky," Holly exclaimed. "You have a good shot at winning the title if the waves are pumping."

"And a swell is on the rise that's supposed to be overhead by tomorrow," Bethany added.

"Then you have it cinched!" said Monica.

"Except, I am not sure I should go," Bethany countered.

"What? Are you crazy? This is for the amateur title," said Holly. "This is what you have been working hard for all year! The waves are not going to be sloppy mush-burgers, so you have a more than better chance of acing the contest!"

"Yeah, Bethany. Why in the world would you even consider *not* going to this contest?" Jenna asked, confused. "We all know how disappointed you were when you didn't make the cut."

Bethany sat on the edge of the bunk and lowered her head.

"You made a promise to Eduardo, didn't you?" Monica asked, suddenly nailing it on the head.

"Yeah," Bethany said slowly. "I told him that I would be there when he woke up from surgery."

"Well, that was *before* you knew you could be in the contest, right?" Holly interjected.

"Yeah, but I don't know if that changes anything," said Bethany.

"Whatd'ya mean? That changes everything! You can just get the word to him that something unexpected came up," Holly said.

"I don't know if I agree with you. What if I made a promise to hang around with you for the afternoon, but then I got invited to hang with someone else, called you up, and cancelled out. How would you feel?"

"Well, I would be upset that you didn't invite me to go with you," Holly replied.

"Holly, I know you! You would be *really* hurt and probably mad too," said Bethany.

"Yeah ... probably," said Holly. "But this is different. This is the amateur title, for heaven's sake!"

"And you can always come back and visit Eduardo after the contest," Jenna offered.

"Plus you have sponsors. You have an obligation to them, don't you?" Holly added.

Bethany felt herself being swayed toward entering the contest by the arguments of her friends. They were right. This was the contest she had been working all year to be a part of. She knew that if the surf was as promised, her odds of winning were strong. Besides, the companies that sponsored her had been more than generous, and she had a responsibility to them. She didn't want to let them down.

Yet deep in her heart Bethany was uneasy with this decision. And she sensed that making the right decision was not going to be easy with her well-meaning friends hovering around her.

"I'm gonna go down to the living room and think about this for a while … by myself."

Bethany left the bunk room and made her way to the living room.

It was dark, but she didn't bother to turn on a light. Through the barred windows she could see the lights of Tijuana spreading over the distant hills. She stared at them for a moment and then slid to one end of a mushy sofa to wrestle through her dilemma.

Lord, I don't know what to do. You gave me the talent to surf and now the opportunity to be in the championship, and yet I don't know what to do! Bethany prayed silently.

Almost immediately, Bethany felt a sense of reassurance that she really did know what to do. Her inner voice told her, *You've known from the very start what to do.*

Suddenly Bethany's mind was drawn back to the horrible day when she was the one lying in the hospital bed. The faces around her included family, friends, surfing buddies, and others who flooded the hospital when they heard the news. People set aside what they were doing because they cared about one little girl who was in a world of hurt.

She heard the echo of Eddie's voice quoting Jesus: " 'I'm telling the solemn truth: Whenever you did one of these things to someone overlooked or ignored, that was me—you did it to me.' "

"Bethany?"

Bethany nearly jumped out of her skin until she realized it was Monica standing in the doorway of the room.

"Yeah?"

"I didn't mean to barge in on you, but I really felt I needed to say something." Monica took a deep breath, and Bethany thought, *Oh, great, here it comes!*

"I just wanted to say that I remember you saying that a person's word—especially a Christian's—should mean something. And you said that if someone made a promise, he or she should keep it." Monica paused and glanced down at her shoes. "Some people in my family don't exactly live like that ... but listening to you ... I don't know ... it made me believe that what you said was right. It sounds crazy, but I think maybe God wanted me to share this with you."

"Not so crazy, Monica. You're probably right."

Bethany had her answer. The surf contest was an opportunity but also a test. A test she could pass and still fail.

"I've gotta call my mom," she said as she pulled herself off the couch and headed for Eddie's office. A thought suddenly occurred to her, and she glanced over her shoulder at Monica.

"Thank you, Monica. You really helped me with this tough decision. I have a feeling God has big plans for you."

"You think so?" Monica said hopefully.

eight

Thick morning fog enveloped the hillsides of Tijuana as Bethany, huddled in her sweatshirt, stood on the porch. She blew out her warm breath, watching as it turned to vapor.

This is so cool, she thought to herself, *you can never see your breath in the tropics!*

The crunch of Eddie's car over the gravel and dirt road announced his arrival before she saw him in the fog.

Maggie was in the front seat, and Bethany piled into the backseat as they pulled up.

"So, no surf contest?" Eddie asked.

"Not for me. I thought about it, but I made a promise to Eduardo, and I think keeping my promise is more important than a surf contest."

"Even the championships?" Maggie said.

"Even the championships," Bethany echoed with a smile. "Besides, I've won contests before. I'll let you in on a secret; it's a big thrill for about twenty minutes. But right after they hand you the trophy, that's it. Nobody cares anymore. They all go home and do other stuff."

"Yeah, I won a contest once," Eddie said as he glanced in the rearview mirror.

"For what? I don't know anything about this," Maggie said, surprised.

"I entered a model-building contest when I was a kid. Took forever making this great model. I won, got a ribbon, and thought I was real hot stuff too. Nobody else seemed all that impressed, though. A few years later when I was a teenager, I tied fire-crackers to my model and blew it up—just for fun."

"And now you live in Mexico where you can get your hands on fireworks anytime you want," Maggie said, and she and Bethany laughed.

Eduardo was not in his bed when Eddie, Maggie, and Bethany arrived. Eduardo's mother told them that he had been taken into surgery an hour before.

The trio sat with Eduardo's mother in the waiting room. Eddie prayed a long prayer in Spanish as his mother softly wept.

Bethany prayed as well—a much shorter but deep prayer from her heart.

Eventually, the boy came out of surgery and was wheeled back to his room.

"It will take him a while to wake up," Eddie said after speaking with the doctor. "How about we go out and get some breakfast and then come back."

Bethany shook her head no. "I'm staying. I told him that I would be here when he woke up."

"Okay, Bethany, you stay here with Eduardo's mother. Maggie and I will bring you both back something to eat."

"All right."

Eduardo's mother and Bethany walked slowly back to Eduardo's room where the boy lay sleeping.

Bethany saw the thickly bandaged leg with the obvious empty place where a foot should have been. She automatically reached up to touch the empty place that had been her arm.

As she took her seat across from Eduardo's mother, Bethany felt the awkwardness of not being able to communicate. She cleared her throat and looked around.

Bethany sensed the woman staring at her, but she didn't make eye contact with her.

After a few minutes of silence punctuated only by Eduardo's breathing, Bethany heard the woman say softly, almost under her breath, "*Tu comprendes*?" And then again, in thickly accented English, "You understand?"

Bethany lifted her head. The little boy's mother was speaking to her but staring at the knotted sleeve on her left shoulder.

"I understand," Bethany nodded.

Eddie and Maggie appeared with a sack of fruit, yogurt, and some pastries.

"Has our buddy awoken yet?" Eddie asked with a hopeful smile.

"Not yet. But I noticed he's moving around a bit more," said Bethany.

"He may need to be on some serious pain medicine for awhile," Maggie said.

"I hope he doesn't feel phantom pain," Bethany said worriedly. "He may feel pain in his foot even though it isn't there. That can happen to people who lose a limb."

Bethany was in the middle of her second banana when she heard Eduardo moan and say, "Mama."

His mother jumped to her feet and reached out to stroke the little boy's hair.

"He's waking up!" Bethany said excitedly.

"Yeah, but he is still kind of out of it," Eddie observed. "It'll probably be a few more hours before he's in the mood to talk."

"Yes, but he is awake, and I promised I'd be here when he woke up."

Bethany slid up near the boy and said his name softly.

Eduardo's eyes turned toward her, and a faint smile flickered across his face.

Then Bethany squeezed Eduardo's hand gently. "I'll be back," she said. "You get strong. I'll be back."

Turning to Eddie, Bethany said, "Okay, Eddie, we can go now. I'm in the mood to build some houses."

nine

Bethany dug her toes into the fine white sand and stared intently at the crisp, dark blue waves zipping along the sandbar.

It was almost a year later, but she and the team where back to the same beach outside of Tijuana where they had once taken the kids from the orphanage.

On the beach, under a small tent, Malia and Jenna were selling T-shirts like hot cakes. The girls, with their artist flair, had created the design and learned how to screen print so they could make the T-shirts themselves.

Small children raced up and down the beach, chased by frantic guardians and nearly colliding with the masses of Americans clustered there as well.

"This is a pretty cool thing you came up with — a Pro/Am surf benefit here at Punta Bandito," said a thickly accented Australian voice from behind Bethany.

It was Bart McClay, the new surfing whiz kid from Down Under who was well on his way to stealing away the world title from its current owner.

"Thanks!" said Bethany.

"You gonna have a go-out before the contest?" Bart asked.

"Yeah, in just a minute," said Bethany.

"Okay then, see you in the water."

Bethany turned back toward the beach and marveled at what she saw.

Huge vendors' tents lined the sand with the judge's tent perched on a small cliff above. Brightly colored flags and banners bearing logos for world-famous surf-related companies fluttered in the gentle offshore wind.

Crowds of people — both Americans and Mexicans — choked the beach. Bethany caught the familiar scent of burning mesquite wood. She grinned. It was a sure sign that a taco vendor had set up shop here.

Soon the guest of honor would arrive, and Bethany knew that if she was going to get in any free-time surfing, she had better do it now.

She reached back to make sure the zipper on her wet suit was cinched up tight and then slipped the leash of her surfboard on her left foot.

As was her custom, she bowed in prayer before wading into the water.

Even though the water was chilly, the wet suit quickly surrounded her with a cushion of warmth.

I can't believe some people have to wear these things all the time, she thought with deep appreciation that she could surf in warm water all year long in Hawaii.

As she stroked into the lineup, she watched as pro surfer after pro surfer—the best in the world—put on a dazzling display of skill, shredding each wave with incredible speed, turns, and gymnastics.

As she paddled to the lineup, she passed Anne Nicholson, now recovered and charging up the ranks of the pro circuit.

"Hey, Anne!"

"Bethany! You put all of this together?" Anne asked appreciatively.

"Well, not really. I mean I had a *lot* of help. In fact, you even helped make this happen."

"What?" said Anne.

"If you hadn't gotten hurt last season, I never would have come up with this idea."

"Whatcha mean? You never took your slot; it went to someone else."

"I know … and it's kind of a long story. Trust me, it all worked out for the best."

"Well, I'm glad to be down here surfing with you."

"Me too, Anne. Me too."

Back on the beach, Bethany's brother Noah had already set up his camera and was recording the blazing ride of each surfer. Her brother Timmy bobbed in the lineup, his own camera in hand, as he watched for the perfect shot.

Under a small tent, Tom and Cheri Hamilton watched Bethany take off on her first wave — a clean, head-high left that unrolled machinelike toward the beach as she carved white tracks up and down its face.

"I'm really proud of that girl," Bethany's dad said. "I always knew she was a great surfer, but I never realized she was such an organizer."

"Well, her heart was in it, Tom. A lot of us find more motivation and drive when we are doing something we are passionate about."

"She sure had lots of help," Tom said. "It seems that many of her friends are passionate about this event too."

"I don't think Sarah and the youth group would've allowed her to do this without them," Cheri said.

After twenty minutes, Bethany caught one last wave, and when it turned to white water, she lay down on her board and let the soup carry her to the beach.

Bethany ran to the van she had come in, grabbed a gallon jug of fresh water from the rear storage compartment, and poured it over her head. Slipping out of her wet suit, she climbed into sweatpants and a light sweatshirt flashing the Rip Curl logo. Then she made her way back to the beach, where she stood next to her parents as she sipped some cold water.

"Where's the guest of honor?" Cheri asked Bethany.

"On the way, I'm sure!" said Bethany. Just as those words came out, Bethany saw Eddie's familiar SUV bouncing along the dirt road.

"They're here!" she called excitedly.

Bethany ran to the parking lot and moved several bright orange cones out of the way. "Over here!" she yelled to Eddie.

The car rolled into the space Bethany had reserved for it, and from out of the back door came several Mexican children followed by Eduardo's mother and finally Eduardo himself.

Bethany could see that he was wearing long pants plus shoes and socks. He walked toward her with barely a limp.

You would never know that he was missing a foot, the way he handles himself, Bethany thought with more than a little admiration for the pint-sized warrior.

Bethany hugged him to herself tightly. She spoke to Eduardo briefly and then glanced up at Eddie and said, "He is doing so well!"

"Better than that! You ought to see him play soccer," Eddie grinned.

"Soccer?" Bethany said, turning back to Eduardo.

"Sí!" beamed the boy who made the motion of kicking a soccer ball with his foot.

"The kids all want him on their team because they think he can kick the ball twice as hard with a steel foot," Eddie laughed.

"Well, now that you are here, we can get this contest underway," Bethany said with a warm smile for her friend Eduardo.

She took Eduardo and his mother around, introducing them to her Kauai *ohana*, or family and friends, as well as every shining light of the professional surf industry that happened to be on hand.

Soon the loudspeakers began to blare an announcement in both English and Spanish: "Ladies and gentlemen, we are pleased to welcome you to the Punta Bandito Pro/Am Charity Surf Expo. We are pleased that you are here and want you to know that the proceeds from all fees, concession booths, and product sales will join the generous donations being made by the sponsors of this event. Now, please give a warm welcome to the originator of today's expo who is here to say a few words to us—Miss Bethany Hamilton."

Bethany, in spite of the many speaking opportunities since the shark attack, still felt far more comfortable dropping in on a huge pitching wave than she did speaking into a microphone. She stood nervously and said, "Thank you for your support. The money we raise here is going to a special fund to help poor children of Tijuana get medical treatment they couldn't afford otherwise. I really appreciate all my friends in the surfing world helping me to do this for these children."

Wild applause and whistles followed Bethany's little speech, and she blushed deeply at the attention.

For the rest of the day, a carnival atmosphere took over the beach. Pro surfers signed autographs after their surf sessions, and sponsors loaded up every child with T-shirts, hats, stickers, and posters.

Eduardo and his family, who had *never* been to the beach, kept getting lost in the crowd. Several times Bethany had to hunt Eduardo down so she could introduce him to various surf stars and VIPs of surf companies.

Eduardo, for his part, was wide-eyed in a world he had never heard about or seen before. Just the sight of the waves, the smell of the ocean, and the feel of the salty sea breeze was enough to send him on sensation overload. It was as if he was in the middle of an aquatic Disneyland.

As the afternoon wore on, a tall man with graying hair and a bright aloha shirt approached Bethany and Eduardo. "*Cómo estás?*" he said to the boy while squatting down and extending a hand. He spoke to Eduardo for a few minutes in Spanish. Then he stood up and turned to Bethany. "Hello, Bethany," the stranger said kindly. "My name is Bob Jensen, and I wanted to be part of this event for a couple reasons. I'm a surfer, but I'm a doctor as well. I specialize in orthopedic recovery for children like Eduardo."

He pulled a business card out of his pocket and handed it to Bethany. "When you get a chance, give me a call, and I will arrange to have this boy fitted with the best kind of prosthetic foot available."

"Really?" Bethany studied the man's face, not quite believing what she had heard.

"Really," he said with a kind smile. "Eduardo's wound is the kind that has a great prognosis for the kind of prosthetics being made today. I would guess that within a few months he could do just about anything anyone with two normal feet could do: run, jump, swim, and even surf!"

"Play competitive soccer?" Bethany prompted.

"Absolutely! No problem at all."

"Wow! Thank you!" said Bethany. "Can you tell Eduardo what you just told me?"

"Sure." He bent down and spoke to the little boy. Eduardo smiled and patted the man's cheek, saying something that apparently startled the doctor. Bethany saw his eyes well up with tears.

"What did Eduardo say to you?"

Dr. Jensen turned to her, cleared his throat, and smiled a trembly smile. "He said he thinks he knows what God's face looks like now."

"What?" asked Bethany with surprise.

The doctor shrugged as he nodded. He looked shaken as he tapped his card in Bethany's hand

and reminded her, "Don't forget to call." Then he slowly walked away.

"No, I won't forget!" Bethany called after him and then glanced back at Eduardo who was smiling up at her with the most beautiful smile she had ever seen. *I won't ever forget this day!*

As the sun began its final plunge toward the ocean, the banners were rolled up, tents collapsed, and a tired but happy group of kids slowly trudged through the mostly empty parking lot toward their van.

"Well, this has been a remarkable day," Eddie said to Bethany and Maggie as they walked behind the children. Eddie and Maggie's ministry had been given a large check to use to help children with medical needs.

"When I came to Mexico last year, I was expecting to be the one who was helping others," Bethany said with a smile. "Instead, I feel like I was the one who learned a lot."

"Yeah?" Eddie said, turning to look at her.

"Well, it was a real surprise to me to learn that being a person who sticks to her word costs a lot. I mean, I never expected it to be that much of a personal struggle."

Eddie and Maggie remained silent, and Bethany continued.

"I can see now how God really used that lesson for the greater good. I mean, I'm so glad we had this opportunity to help Eduardo and kids like him.

I might have missed all that if I had gone back on my promise."

"Well, like I always say, if a man doesn't have his word, he doesn't have anything," Eddie said. "I'm glad you were able to figure that out."

"But there's a lot more I came to understand too," Bethany rushed on excitedly.

"I learned that I really admire people like you two. I hang out with people who are stars in the world of surfing. You saw it today. These people have everything: kids asking for their autographs, T-shirts with their pictures or names on them, and photos and articles about them in magazines. But to be honest, I think you guys are the real stars."

"Aw," Eddie said, brushing away the compliment with a wave of his hand.

"Seriously, people have it all backward! They put the wrong people on the covers of magazines."

"Well, Bethany, God has it all figured out, and he has all of eternity to do it. Like Jesus said, 'Many who are first will be last, and many who are last will be first' and 'Whoever exalts himself will be humbled, and whoever humbles himself will be exalted.' "

"What do you say we get in line for some tacos tonight—the Hamiltons' treat," said Bethany.

"There's always room for tacos!" Eddie laughed.

That evening at a corner taco stand in Tijuana where the exhaust fumes from speeding cars mixed with the sound of honking horns, Eddie,

Maggie, Eduardo, and his mother and siblings joined the Hamilton family for a feast.

"Here's how you do it, Dad," Bethany explained. "You order however many you want and whatever you want to drink. Then, when you are all done eating, you simply tell the guy how many tacos and drinks you had, and he will tell you how much you owe."

"Isn't he afraid of getting ripped off?" Tom asked, a little surprised. "What if we were to try to cheat him by saying we had three tacos when we had six?"

"Dad, there are some places in the world where the word of a person still means something. Don't worry; he will trust you. He knows you are a Christian."

Bethany smiled at Eddie and Maggie, and they smiled back.

"You must have a good name here," Tom said.

"It's the result of lots and lots of honest dealings with other believers," Bethany said.

"Hmm, reminds me of a verse," Cheri said, smiling. "A good name is more desirable than great riches; to be esteemed is better than silver or gold."

"I think I'll have another taco on that note," Bethany said happily.

Body and Soul

A Girl's Guide to a Fit, Fun and Fabulous Life

Bethany Hamilton
with Dustin Dillberg

Bethany Hamilton has become a fitness expert by virtue of being a professional athlete who has excelled—and she's done it while overcoming incredible challenges. In *Body & Soul*, a total wellness book for girls ages 8 and up, Bethany shares some of her own experiences while helping young girls gain confidence and develop a pattern of healthy living starting at a young age. In addition to workouts and recipes, Bethany also shares her unstoppable faith and emphasizes how spiritual health is just as important as physical health.

Includes:

- Workouts specially developed for young girls by Bethany's personal trainer
- Recipes and information on healthy eating based on "Bethany's food pyramid," which follows the Mediterranean diet
- Advice on deepening your spiritual health and total body wellness

Available in stores and online!

Soul Surfer Series

Clash

*Rick Bundschuh, Inspired
by Bethany Hamilton*

Book one in the Soul Surfer Series

Burned

*Rick Bundschuh, Inspired
by Bethany Hamilton*

Book two in the Soul Surfer Series

Storm

*Rick Bundschuh, Inspired
by Bethany Hamilton*

Book three in the Soul Surfer Series

Crunch

*Rick Bundschuh, Inspired
by Bethany Hamilton*

Book four in the Soul Surfer Series

Available in stores and online!

ZONDER**kidz**